The Phantom Returns

Stefanie Cole

Copyright © 2007 by Stefanie Cole

JimSam Inc.
P.O. Box 3363
Riverview, FL 33568
www.JimSamInc.com

All rights reserved. No part of this publication may be reproduced, stored in a retrieval system or transmitted, in any form, or by any means, electronic, mechanical, recorded, photocopied, or otherwise, without the prior permission of the copyright owner, except by a reviewer who may quote brief passages in a review.

Printed in the United States of America

Cover by Samantha Kellenberger

ISBN: 978-0-9790768-4-8

A Note of Thanks

To my beautiful son who refers to the Phantom as "Eyebrow"
~
To Therese and Pam, my angels of editing, who took this new author and her story under their talented wings ~

To my incredibly supportive family, hopefully there will be more books to come for separate dedications! I love you ~

To my awesome phriends ~ Lottie, Nightsmusic, Mooky, Sereenie, Jomas, Ayesha, Jayro, Redrose, Angeleyes, Nana, Rem, KFC, GOG, Cheri, Marbs, Mia, Marilyn, Kitty, Pho4ph, PMA, Phanna, Cantrell, Carousel, Crayann, MAO, DXH, Bochis, Amused, MissPhantom, Neice, ~ Your Diva ees pleased! (and so sorry she could not fit everyone on this list!)

*Applause to Rappleyea for her verse ~

Special Thanks to ~ Maria, Marcia, and Sam who helped my dream come true. And to Judy who did a great homerun-stretch edit for me!

Your Humble and Obedient Diva,
S.C.

Foreword

ASUMPTUOUS lair lies underneath a fashionable Opera House in Paris. At one time the lair, though set in a cavernous grotto far underground, was as magnificent to behold as the Opera House itself. Above and below, smooth, ivory candles burned brightly. Powerful music flowed through the rooms. Lavish touches of gilt and velvet filled every corner. But now both the Opera House and the lair sit disturbingly vacant.

To walk into the Opera House is to do so at your own peril, as this establishment has suffered a devastating fire.

To venture down, down, into the bowels of the Opera House and discover the hidden lair is to find that devastation has made its presence known here as well. But, if you stop for a moment, close your eyes, and let yourself absorb, you feel it is a devastation of a different sort, that of the heart and soul.

Lives have been lost in this Opera House; a life was spared in the underground lair.

The tale on which you are about to embark continues from the tragic love triangle of The Phantom of the Opera. A young, orphaned girl named Christine came to this very Opera House at the age of seven. Guided and mothered by the formidable dance instructor, Madame Giry, taken under the Angel of Music's wing and given the gift of song, soon her entire being existed for music and her Angel, who, unbeknownst to Christine also went by another name.

For many years, the Opera House suffered under the mysterious curse of an Opera Ghost, a Phantom of the Opera if you will, who is said to have existed in the darkest corners of people's minds and the deepest shadows of the establishment. No one had ever seen this specter, yet all who worked under the roof of this Opera House obeyed his commands without fail. They paid his fees, left his box seat vacant for his use alone, and turned a blind eye when things disappeared. Only Madame Giry knew the truth of the Opera Ghost's past and present, for much as she had brought Christine in this world of dance and song, Madame Giry had also led a young, disfigured boy through these same walls many years ago—the boy who would someday turn into the feared Opera Ghost.

The secret lessons held in a chapel created a sense of singular closeness with the two lost souls, but music forged the unbreakable bond between the Angel, a compelling teacher and the girl, his enthralled student.

Yet, while the girl danced freely in the light, surrounded by her friends and fellow performers, her Angel composed his melodies in the bottomless dark, imprisoned in solitude by his deformity.

As Christine grew to womanhood, she became part of the ballet corps of the Opera House, dancing in public, and singing in secret, versed by her Angel. Christine never knew that her beloved Angel of Music and the menacing Opera Ghost were one and the same. And perhaps, if her childhood sweetheart, the Vicomte de Chagny, had not come into the picture as a patron of the Opera House, she might never have learned the truth.

From there the madness took hold. The Vicomte's presence pushed the Phantom to make himself known and declare his devotion for Christine. In his desperation at the thought of losing her, his pursuit grew violent and obsessive. Christine, unable to accept the fact that this monster and her Angel were one and the same, turned to the safe haven of Raoul de Chagny's arms. The Opera Ghost's wrath knew no limitations, including murder.

Christine and Raoul fled the burning Opera House, away

from the clutches of The Phantom of the Opera.

They are married now; and with their new roles, they struggle to find their place in Raoul's privileged world of the aristocracy. Christine tries to fulfill her title as the new Vicomtesse and ignore the disquieting emptiness in her heart since leaving the Phantom, while her husband experiences the unforeseen trials of marrying a common girl of no title and battles the growing unease in his soul.

Or perhaps they struggle, because they both know without any proof given, that the Phantom of the Opera did not die that night in his lair; that their star-crossed story is not yet over. That he is somewhere out there, watching and waiting...for his second chance with Christine.

> **Loss** a: the act of losing possession b: the harm or privation resulting from loss or separation
> **Redemption** a: to free from the consequences of sin b: to change for the better
> **Love** a: the object of attachment, devotion, or admiration b: unselfish loyal and benevolent concern for the good of another

Chapter 1

THE house rested on a cliff overlooking a moody ocean, underneath the ever-changing sky. Old and drafty, it nevertheless contained a textured resonance of many memories. Laughter, love, and finally death had played out within these walls. And Christine de Chagny, formerly Christine Daae, had been the bright thread that wove these memories together.

She stood on the threshold of her childhood home, the only home she remembered before going to live at the Opera House. Almost ten years ago, she had left this dwelling after her father died. And much as her father was, she thought the house lost to her forever. Yet now, thanks to her new husband, she found herself once again in this haven of her youth.

Christine hoped Raoul felt as elated as she; as a boy, this place had been a retreat for him away from the repressive confines of the Chateau de Chagny, a neighboring property. Together, they spent many hours outside, conjuring up bold adventures, or when Mother Nature's disposition turned foul, pilfering food from the kitchen and tucking themselves away in the attic to read tales of enchantment.

Heavy sheets now covered what was left of the furniture; dust motes danced in weak shafts of sunlight let in by grimy windows; a breeze from the open doorway caused cobwebs to cling and shiver in their corners.

Christine saw herself, as a carefree girl of five, sitting on the floor by her father's knee while he played a new song on his violin. Smoke from his ever-present pipe gave off a rich, comforting scent that Christine loved.

He laid his bow against the strings and winked at his daughter.

"Dance for me, my littlest angel?"

And while the violin played its spirited tune, Christine threw her dimpled hands high up in the air, twirling and twirling in front the crackling fire, until the jaunty, red ribbon that her father could never tie tightly enough came loose and her brown curls flew about her shoulders. He would not stop playing until she landed in a heap on the braided carpet, laughing and out of breath.

"What the devil?" Raoul came up behind her. "I sent orders ahead to have this house cleaned and stocked for our arrival. I am sorry, this place is filthy."

"No, Raoul, it is perfect." she whispered.

The sound of an approaching carriage brought a look of satisfaction to Raoul's face. The servants and supplies had finally arrived. "Now, it is perfect, Christine."

Wrapped in her husband's arms at night and captivated with the rediscovery of her childhood home and the land around it, Christine spent her honeymoon in a blissful state. She convinced herself that she had emotionally healed and would be able to lead a contented existence by Raoul's side, laying aside all thoughts of her Angel.

During this time of newly wedded harmony, only one ripple disturbed the clear, smooth waters of the young couple's time. Christine had wandered into her father's music room and discovered a treasure. In a nondescript wooden box, tucked away in an old chest of drawers, she found scores of music. Her father had written some; well-known composers created others and Christine had listened to them all, first as a child and later at the Opera House. As she leafed through the compositions, lost in happy recollection, she came upon a particular title that caused her to let out a short gasp of recognition—*The Angel of Music*!

This song signaled the fateful crossing of Christine's old life into the new. She stared at the lyrics, dumbfounded. *The Angel of Music* had been the first piece she had sung at the Opera House. It symbolized the initial bond between Christine and her mentor. The title created a name for her unseen companion. But stranger than she could comprehend, the twist to this finding lay in the fact that though her father had owned this piece of music also, he had never played it for her.

Christine studied the paper trying to glean more information and discovered some unknown composer had written the tune over a century ago. She struggled to place her memories in sequence if only to marginally understand what she suspected lay beyond her scope.

Before her father died, he had promised to send her an Angel of Music. Her father kept this song a secret, but it obviously meant a great deal to him. It held enough power that on his deathbed, he believed that these lyrics could come to life. This promise provided the singular comfort to a girl who in mere hours would become an orphan. Christine blinked away the moisture that welled under her lids and let her mind journey back to her first days at the Opera House, when her father's promise came true. For soon after his death, Christine had learned the words, heard the music, found her angel—a fallen angel, but an angel all the same.

She sat on the icy stone floor of the simple chapel, adjacent to the Opera House. Her fifth day in the noisy arena where privacy could only be attained within her own mind, Christine found a niche of peace, away from the irreverent occupants of the Opera House. Every day thus far, Christine performed the same ritual. She lit a candle in front of the daguerreotype of her father and murmured a quiet, heartfelt prayer to his memory and then she waited. She waited for the nightmare to end, waited for her father to come back, waited for his promise to come true. A seven-year-old girl so well-loved, who still heard her father's music in her heart, could believe no less. Christine sat for hours inside the chapel, unwilling to leave until Madame Giry's sharp voice called down the corridor.

"Christine Daae, it is time for supper. I will send Meg to fetch you if you do not return from the chapel at once."

That evening, as she struggled to her feet, knees stiff, limbs cold, the dim chapel brightened and Christine looked automatically to the large stained glass window. Set in the midst of all the paneled shapes and hues of the glass, stood a beautifully wrought angel, which to Christine's mind, now seemed to radiate warmth and love. And while Christine closed her eyes and let the myriad of colors play against her face, she listened, without surprise, to a lilting melody, sung in a haunting voice that infused the room with glory. Her Angel of Music had come and though she could not see him, it did not matter, for with the sheer presence of his voice alone, Christine knew solitude no more.

Now, standing here holding this music, thinking back on her past, Christine acknowledged that there were powers in the world that did not adhere to her normal religious beliefs. Before her father had been born, a simple song had been composed, its existence made known to those whose fates were bound within the words.

Caught amidst these powerful musings, feeling far removed from the present, Christine cleared her throat, ignoring the inner voice of caution against singing this song, against singing at all.

> Lyrical Angel, Watch over me
> Or lost and alone, forever I'll be
>
> Lyrical Angel, sing me to sleep
> Close by me, beside me, your secrets I'll keep
>
> Lyrical Angel, my heart is devout
> Your song, your guidance, I cannot live without
>
> Lyrical Angel, my mirror, my soul
> To choose another, I would not be—

"What are you doing?" Raoul's harsh tone shattered the melody.

Christine unconsciously pressed the papers against her chest. "I was singing, Raoul. I found some of father's old scores and it felt lovely to—"

Raoul scoffed, "Christine, you do not need to sing for your supper any longer. You are a Vicomtesse." He strode to her and plucked the sheets from her grasp; for one second Christine clasped the papers tighter, and then released them without a fight.

She watched sadly as Raoul carelessly stuffed the music inside the box and flinched as he shut the lid with a bang. "Those papers are important to me, Raoul; they are part of my history—not only with my father, but with the Opera House as well. It is an enormous part of who I am…my entire past."

Raoul's mouth thinned, a clear sign of his displeasure, of which Christine had never before been the recipient. "Christine, to be perfectly honest with you, I do not understand the need to speak of your life at the Opera House when you have such a promising future as my wife." His glance fell on the wooden box and his voice roughened. "I thought I had lost you to the Opera Ghost. I almost *died* at the hands of that hideous madman. I am afraid I cannot discuss any aspect of that time without remembering the horror and the pain, and I cannot believe that you would expect that of me!"

Flailing in the storm of his eyes, Christine tried to apologize. "I did not think. I am sorry, Raoul." Christine saw these words were not enough to soothe her husband and her mind sought some stronger means of placating him. "No thoughts within my head, but thoughts of song. *He* is not a part of me any longer, I swear."

Why, oh why did this feel like perfidy to her Angel's memory? Christine had opened the wooden box too soon into her marriage, and Raoul had shut the box too late to erase the impact of such soul wrenching memories. No matter how tightly latched the lid, a change had occurred within Christine while she sang; her heart felt a little fuller. Someone or something had taken up residence inside, and it terrified her to recognize its existence.

Raoul mistook her great agitation for remorse on his behalf and sought to calm her. He gathered her in his arms. "I believe you, Christine. I should have known better than to sully our honeymoon by speaking of that *creature*. There is only you and I, and the past cannot hurt us."

Christine let herself be held, finding a measure of comfort in

Raoul's warmth, if not his words. She never believed that particular phrase, for, if anything, the past had the absolute power to resurface and alter a person's life, for good or bad.

As they quitted the music room hand in hand, Christine tucked this lesson away, now aware that discussing the years before her marriage would never be allowed. Was she to have two identities now? That of Christine Daae, naïve chorus girl captivated by an Opera Ghost, and now, Vicomtesse de Chagny, naïve wife with no idea what her husband expected of her?

However she might acquiesce to Raoul's request of sealing her past away, she would not relinquish one part of her history: her friendship with Madame Giry and her daughter, Meg. Madame Giry had taken Christine in at the passing of Christine's father, and Meg was the closest thing Christine had to a sister. Despite any disapproval from Raoul, she was not about to set her relationships with these women aside. Secretly, Christine hoped that her friendship with Meg and Madame would provide the link between Christine Daae and the Vicomtesse de Chagny.

Days rolled by pleasurably. Raoul attended to Christine's every whim, taking care of all decisions, asking nothing from his bride. She knew he wanted this honeymoon to be perfect and lost track of the number of times he made her glow with a romantic phrase or gesture.

At the end of three months, the newlyweds arrived at Raoul's estate in Paris, floating on a cloud of youthful love.

Upon their return, the reality of being wife to a Vicomte grounded Christine in a most unpleasant manner.

16 months later...

Another act to perform. Christine felt her palms dampen inside the white opera length gloves she wore. As she climbed the steps toward the entrance, she prayed that her reception in London as the Vicomtesse de Chagny would result in success rather than the unexpected failure she suffered in Paris.

Christine shot a sidelong look at her husband, sensing that this ball and how she would be received concerned him as much as it did her.

Neither she nor Raoul had foreseen the ill regard for their hasty marriage, or that a union with the beautiful, accomplished Christine Daae of the Opera House would be a detriment to her husband's social standing.

Raoul gave her arm a reassuring squeeze, startling Christine out of her reverie. She saw him glance at her troubled countenance as they moved forward in the short line of people waiting to be announced. She swiftly put on her social smile and straightened her spine.

"Do not worry, my love. The English will adore you." Raoul kept his voice low as he lightly teased, "They will fall under an immediate enchantment when you cast those wondrous brown eyes of yours at them—just as I did."

Christine studied Raoul, her gilded-haired knight, looking so earnest and handsome in his evening attire. She wanted to tell him that she worried for him, that she wished that their marriage weren't causing such a rift with his friends. But Christine merely held her smile and tried to match his mood with her own attempt at levity. "Oh yes, a chorus girl with the scandal of murder attached to her name."

They moved closer to the entryway, and Raoul clasped her gloved hand. "You are much more than that. So much more!" Christine arched her brows at the raised level of Raoul's tone, and he swiftly lowered it again. "I tried to bring you out in Paris society too soon. But I highly doubt that these people will care about an old scandal from across the channel. You are my wife and a Vicomtesse; show these Londoners what an incredible choice I have made. They will love you as I do."

Christine averted her gaze, looking out to the lush rose gardens beyond. She could not bear to let Raoul see the disbelief in her eyes. Not when she could read the unmistakable strain in his. The black and white of the worlds from which they came had already begun to take their toll. Raoul had been born to his title; he lived and breathed this life.

Christine had been born to a life of music, a life that she missed with quiet misery. Just as Raoul could not bring himself to share his difficulties with his wife, Christine knew she must keep silent the fact that she missed the open acceptance and camaraderie of the Opera House, missed her singing, missed…

"The Vicomte and Vicomtesse de Chagny!"

They found themselves on top of the wide staircase leading into a ballroom that glittered with the aristocracy of England. Liveried servants bore small silver trays of champagne, the orchestra played a cheerful minuet, and delicate chairs had been set out for those needing a rest or for dowagers who preferred to keep a close eye on their charges. Christine found nothing different in the setting from any of the Paris balls, including the effect that her presence evoked; she berated herself for having entertained any optimism at all.

People stopped to stare. Christine heard whispers. Saw their eyes gleam with disdain. She looked the part of a Vicomtesse; the dress she wore, a pale blue creation, was in the first stare of fashion. Diamond teardrops hung from her ears. Her long dark brown hair had been styled in a most sophisticated upsweep of curls. Yet, underneath it all, Christine felt a fraud. Without a doubt these haughty strangers thought so as well. London was to be no different from Paris, and Christine wanted nothing more than to turn around and run far, far away. If the gay Parisians had a difficult time accepting Christine…why did Raoul think the English, to whom lineage meant everything, would be any different?

Christine sent a quick, longing look behind her as they descended the staircase into the colorful sea of guests.

"Courage, Little Lotte." Raoul's use of her childhood nickname only served to chip away at her brittle composure.

Raoul led her to a group of men standing with their polished and bejeweled wives. Christine made the acquaintance of two Earls, a Count, and a Baron within seconds. Their eyes assessed her coldly, though their manners were above reproach. Each gentleman gave Christine a polite bow and introduced his wife. Raoul watched the whole exchange intently, and to Christine's dismay, he appeared satisfied with the stiff manners of the men and the saccharine smiles that the women bestowed on her before he turned his attention to talk of hunting. Already of a petite stature, Christine felt even more diminished. A pine sapling in a majestic forest of oaks.

As soon as it became apparent that the Vicomte's interest was absorbed in hounds and horses, the wives made a point to carry on their own conversation as if Christine did not stand within their small circle. Only the Baron's wife paid the Vicomtesse de Chagny any mind: she glared openly, and Christine was all too aware that this woman's resentment lay in the fact that Christine's title exceeded hers.

Suddenly, unable to take in another breath of this oppressive air; Christine excused herself from the group. The women smirked at her departure, delighted to have routed the imposter. Raoul, now immersed in talk of politics, took no notice of her leaving.

Desperate for solitude, Christine made her way to the outskirts of the crowded ballroom; instinct or destiny delivered her to an empty balcony. She leaned on the railing, letting her eyelids drift down. Strains of music filtered out into the starry night, mingling with the heady perfume of the rose gardens. Christine breathed in the scent and the sounds deeply, feeling herself calm for the first time in months. The song she knew well, had danced to it at the Opera House. She longed to sing the words, to express her soul in the effortless beauty of melody. But Christine had learned well her lesson—a Vicomtesse did not sing for pleasure. She sang only to show her worth if it would compliment her husband. So she contented herself by swaying slightly to the music and allowing herself a tiny pocket of blissful indulgence.

Some moments later she realized the orchestra had stopped. Yet the tune went on and still she swayed.

Chapter 2

HE watched her respond to his music, as she had before, as she always would. It went without question that Christine would forever stir his renaissance soul. He continued to hum the melody, remembering simpler times at the Opera House. He felt Christine sense him, and stopped…and waited.

A whisper of wind caressed the back of Christine's neck, lifting a few loose curls. She scanned the balcony and saw him standing in the shadow of the wall, a dark figure on a moonlit night.

It never crossed Christine's mind that the man could be anyone else but her Phantom. The rich tapestry of emotions that rose so quickly inside her just knowing he lingered near overwhelmed her, and Christine grew frightened that Raoul, merely inside the ballroom, already seemed so very far away.

The clouds moved past the moon, revealing his figure in its light and bathing Christine's face. She heard an intake of breath, then, "Oh…Christine." A reverent whisper.

Eyes closed, Christine let his achingly familiar voice flow into her. Felt his fingertips stroke her cheek for an instant. She opened her eyes in time to catch a glimpse of the bittersweet tenderness in his fathomless gaze. A swift flourish of his ebony cape, then he was gone.

A red rose lay on the stone where he had stood, a small note attached to it with a white silk ribbon.

*"Should you ever need me,
I am here for you, sweet Christine"
Erik*

"Erik," she breathed. A man's name had been given to her Phantom. "Erik."

"Christine?" Raoul stood in the opened doorway of the balcony. "Who are you talking to?"

Christine swiftly hid the note in the folds of her gown. The rose, she let slip to the ground behind her as she crossed to Raoul.

"I-I was talking to myself. There aren't many other conversations in which I'm included."

She linked her arm through her husband's, the note hidden in her other hand. Her remark, intended to be light, had stumbled out forced and jittery.

Raoul brought Christine's hand to his lips, his sky-blue eyes earnest and appealing. "I apologize for staying away so long. I haven't seen these friends in some time. Forgive me?"

Christine smiled and nodded. Her eyes glanced for a fraction of a second over to where the rose lay. She couldn't bring herself to tell him. *Forgive me*, she asked silently of Raoul and clutched the note tighter.

As they left the balcony, Raoul made a show of brushing a piece of lint from his evening coat. He looked to where Christine's eyes had darted moments ago. Not a single emotion showed on his face as he walked back into the ballroom with his wife on his arm. Not a single person, including his wife, would be able to tell that the Vicomte de Chagny's heart pounded with fire and fear.

Their thoughts, though never spoken, were identical. *The Phantom has returned.*

⚊

Christine found herself wandering from room to room in their rented townhouse trying to escape one disturbing thought. Two days of unspoken questions and silent confessions had filled the atmosphere of their life since the night of the ball. Then, without warning, Raoul left for Paris, telling her he had an important meeting with his man of affairs that he could not put off. Christine accepted his pithy explanation without comment, thankful to have some time alone to examine her emotions.

Lying to Raoul went against her very nature, yet she could not bring herself to speak of the encounter on the balcony and the turbulent wake it had left behind in her soul, when she had not even begun to sort it out in her mind.

Prior to his leaving, Raoul gifted her with a gold locket. Inside he had tucked likenesses of Christine and himself.

"I'll cherish this, Raoul. Thank you." Christine threw her arms around his neck.

"I love you, Little Lotte. No words can express that enough." Raoul held Christine; his arms wrapped around her like iron bands until he finally released her. His boots crunched heavily on the gravel as he walked away. Christine retreated into the house, unaware that Raoul had stopped or that his eyes followed her until she closed the door behind her.

That had been three days ago. Christine visited no one; no one called on her. Even the servants kept to themselves as they went about their work in the silent house.

Finally, she sat down in the nearest chair and allowed the name to surface. Erik. Her Angel of Music had found and bewildered her with his tender attentions. A memory forced its way up, and she recalled the last painful image she had of him before the other night, desolate and broken in his underground lair as she fled with Raoul. She had kissed her Angel once, of her own volition, because she could not help herself, and she kissed him a second time to show him what it meant to love, and that second kiss had set her… free.

Christine touched her fingertips to her lips. Never once had she forgotten the feel of his mouth on hers or the great burst of rapture in her heart each time their lips met. She had never forgotten the panic she experienced when she realized she harbored such feelings for a murderer. So she ran away with Raoul, whom she loved sweetly. Whom she knew contained no darkness.

Raoul saved her that night, sheltered her when he married her and had protected her ever since. Because of this, Christine experienced overwhelming pangs of conscience for allowing her wayward mind to travel back into this forbidden territory.

Yet, how could she not? After her unsuccessful debut here in London and Erik's untimely arrival, she could not shut out the thought that plagued her incessantly—she had left behind the world to which she really belonged. With the exception of an egocentric Prima Donna, Christine had flourished under the easy acceptance and jovial natures of her fellow performers. She had a place in that world, where others liked her no matter what her name. When she used her talents they fed her soul.

She served no purpose in Raoul's household, had no pastimes to express her artistic nature. Her role as the Vicomtesse de Chagny felt as barren and fallow as the cracked earth of a garden without rain.

To make matters worse, Christine had no one with whom to discuss these sad musings. Even if Raoul were here by her side, Christine knew he would offer no compassion on this taboo subject.

She thought of writing a letter to Madame Giry. But what would she write? That she loved her husband but once again thoughts of The Phantom consumed her? Christine jumped out of the chair and hastened to her room, as if by moving so quickly she might escape her mind's reach. She paused outside her husband's door, and though she had every right to enter, Christine crept furtively inside.

Decorated in blues and golds, Raoul's chambers bespoke of restrained luxury. By an unspoken arrangement, Christine customarily received him in her own bedroom and now looked about curiously, not knowing what she hoped to glean from her absent husband's belongings. She crossed to his wardrobe and opened the doors. Clothing hung in precise lines, and Christine smiled at the vast array of jackets and shirts. Raoul did not stint when it came to his attire.

One after another, Christine ran her hand along the items, trying to get a sense of the man who had become something of a stranger to her at times. Yet, only ghost of familiarity haunted the wardrobe, a shade of her Raoul behind the title. As she closed the wardrobe, the scent of his cologne reached out to pervade her senses in a puff of air. With a dissatisfied sigh, Christine went to her own room.

She dismissed her maid, Simone, then selected a small number of outfits and laid them out on the bed, all the while preoccupied with the unformulated plan in her mind. Christine told herself that three days was too long with no word from her husband. She told herself she was going to Paris to find him. She told herself many things. As she made the short voyage to France, possessed of only a small traveling bag, she prayed that Madame Giry would be at home.

Madame Giry's suite of apartments reflected her distinguished taste. Though her features were cast in austere lines, her mouth constantly set in a straight, unforgiving pinch of crimson, and her snapping eyes, like polished beads of jet, held fast their hard, assessing stare; she had a French woman's eye for whimsical style when it came to decorating. Her furniture consisted of well-chosen pieces that allowed for comfort as well as grace, and she displayed her prized collection of porcelain figures with precise care. To the surprise of most who had the distinction of an invite, Madame's favorite color, used in almost every room, was a soft, sweet, rose.

Her association with Erik had contained many violent turns and soul-wrenching twists. But he had taken care of Madame financially when the bones in her ankle shattered after a burning piece of timber had fallen on her in the Opera House fire, and she lacked for nothing.

She did not blame Erik for anything that had happened to her. She chose her fate, whatever it might be, long ago on the night she had rescued him from an angry mob. He had been such a young boy, then, with such old eyes. The great cruelty she had seen meted against him evoked her pity. The complete lack of hope in his distorted young face pressed her to save him. For years he lived underneath the Opera House, creating and composing, while she lived above, dancing and instructing. A strange relationship, yet it worked for them.

And then their carefully balanced world fell apart upon the arrival of the Vicomte. Madame Giry had tried to explain it to her daughter.

"Love can turn even the sanest of men into lunatics." She hoped that Meg never forgot that lesson. She hoped Christine would not have occasion to remember it.

She had not seen Erik in well over a year, until his unexpected appearance on her doorstep under the blanket of darkness, wearing a mask of white and a cape of midnight.

"Where is Christine?" Erik made no attempt to hide his purpose.

A halfhearted argument ensued as Madame Giry tried to point out the flaws in his plan.

"Monsieur, have you forgotten that you are wanted by the law?"

Erik brushed it aside. "Where is Christine?"

With a touch of desperation, she responded. "Christine is a married woman!"

Erik's eyes blazed. "Where is Christine?"

At her wit's end, Madame insisted. "Perhaps she will not wish to see you."

Erik gave her a broken smile. "That, I shall have to find out for myself."

Madame watched as he stood there, a powerful figure striving for patience. Rolling her eyes to the heavens, she went to her desk and wrote down Christine's address and held it out. "We have corresponded these past two years. Things have changed within her and around her. Please, have a care."

Erik took the note and ran his finger slowly over the writing. "With my last breath."

He nodded at Madame and swept back out into the shadows. Madame Giry absently watched the flames reduce thick logs of wood into cinders…She wondered if it was to be a romance or a tragedy for Erik and Christine.

There would be a loss suffered, that much was certain.

―――

A fortnight passed and her second guest arrived. Raoul pounded heavily on Madame Giry's door. "Madame Giry! Please, open this door at once!"

"Vicomte de Chagny. It has been some time. Please come in." Madame walked away, her slight limp a reminder of the past they all shared.

"He is back. Are you harboring that murdering creature here?" Raoul stood much like Erik had, filled with determination, waiting for an answer.

Madame calmly sat down in her favorite chair. A small table in front of her held an ornate tea service set for two, as if she had been expecting a visitor. She had no news for the Vicomte, nor would she embarrass either of them with pretense, but she prided herself on being a considerate hostess. "Would you care for some tea, Monsieur?"

"No, I would not! He is wanted for murder! May I remind you that you could have gone to prison because of your *association* with him? I shielded you from the law before; I do not think I can do so again if you choose not to assist me."

Madame poured some of the steaming brew into a delicate cup. "Blackmail, Monsieur? Perhaps we have all changed in the past two years."

Raoul drew himself up and crushed his gloves within his fist, clearly affronted with the term blackmail. "Changed, Madame? Are you implying that our monster has changed?"

Only the slightest purse of her lips showed any acknowledgement to his question. Madame Giry sipped her tea. "I am afraid that your visit here serves no purpose. I am sorry I cannot help you, Vicomte."

Her words unmistakably defined their positions, and Raoul turned to leave. "You once helped me save Christine. I pray that your lack of aid this time does not result in her death!"

Madame Giry sat with great composure and maintained her silence. Raoul stormed outside, slamming the door as he went. A delicate figurine of an opera singer wobbled precariously on a nearby shelf. Madame Giry watched it, holding her breath. After tilting back and forth a few more times, the figurine righted itself. Madame exhaled, she wondered how many days it would take before Christine arrived. The answer was four.

―――

"Vicomtesse de Chagny, how well you look."

Christine removed her gloves and cloak, smiling widely at Madame Giry. "Vicomtesse? Madame, I am still the same girl that couldn't remember the difference between a *'Pas de Chat'* and a *'Pas de Deux'*."

Madame frowned at that. "For your sake I hope that is not true, Christine. So, tell me about London. I have not received any letters from you since your arrival there."

Christine followed Madame to the sitting room, prepared to open her soul to her friend, to tell her everything.

In a small adjoining parlor, Erik rested his forehead against the closed door. She had come! Her voice, the clear loveliness of her voice was at once the same and yet so much more. Adrenaline coursed through his veins. He had been right in returning to France after making himself known to her at the ball. Now he knew that she still cared for him, and that feeling had brought her all the way to Madame Giry's doorstep. He wanted to rush in to spirit Christine away! He reached for the doorknob, and then stopped, battling his urges. *For where had these urges taken him before?* his mind demanded. Erik dropped his hand to his side and continued listening to the conversation in the next room. This time her love would be a gift, given freely, or not at all.

Shoulders tensed, Madame Giry could almost feel Erik's will permeate the four walls of the sitting room. *Please, let him wait. Let him listen.* As Christine concluded her story with Raoul's departure, Madame rose from her seat. "So. Where does this leave Christine?"

Christine looked at her helplessly. "I'm not certain."

"You are not certain? That is not nearly good enough! Stand up."

Christine stood up, years of training under Madame not allowing any other option. Madame placed herself in front of Christine, held her shoulders firmly and looked into Christine's eyes.

"You must go now."

"Go? Madame Giry, I do not understand…"

"Exactly. I thought your coming here meant you had the answers, not because you were looking for them from me. And not because you are too afraid to make this kind of choice for yourself."

"I am married, I love Raoul…you don't know what you're asking of me!"

"I am asking of you, Christine? It is not I asking anything—It is not even Erik. His arrival back in your life has only caused the questions that lay buried in your heart to finally resurface and demand answers."

Madame Giry gave Christine a brief embrace that softened the blow. "This is not an easy path. It never has been, but the journey that you started as a girl you must finish as a woman. Now, go. I will tell Meg you send your greetings."

Christine swallowed with difficulty. She donned her cloak and gloves slowly, and like two others before her, exited Madame Giry's apartments conflicted.

As she stood on the threshold in the lengthening shadows of the evening, a voice floated on the wind. "Christine."

Such longing carried in that last syllable and Christine at once responded in kind. "Erik…"

Silence answered her and her driver showed no signs of having heard the whispered exchange. Christine gave the address of her husband's estate and climbed into the carriage. She quickly settled herself into the thick squabs of her seat and let out a troubled sigh as the carriage began to move.

"Little Lotte wondered, whom do I love? Is it a disfigured demon or my faithful husband…?"

"Raoul!" Christine's eyes widened in alarmed surprise.

Raoul leaned forward from the dim confines of the opposite seat. "Do I continue to lie to my husband or do I tell him the truth and put and end to this madness?" His soft voice held a hint of sadness He leaned closer still and held Christine's chin with a gentle hand. "Tell me, Little Lotte, did you find what you were looking for?"

The carriage rumbled on toward the dwelling of the Vicomte and Vicomtesse de Chagny.

Chapter 3

INSIDE Madame's parlor, the door crashed open. "You sent her away! Why?"

Madame faced Erik, unruffled. "You know why."

Erik overturned a chair. "She came to find me! Damn you!"

Madame Giry looked at the chair. "Please pick that up, Monsieur."

Erik stared at the chair, his jaw clenched. He yanked the chair upright and set it in its place. "My apologies, Madame. It has been some time since I have lost my temper. Perhaps the monster is not quite tamed after all." He sat down holding his head in his hands.

"That was not the monster I just witnessed. It was the man—a man who loves deeply."

"Too deeply," came the tortured reply.

Madame laid a tentative hand on his shoulder, the first physical contact she had made with him in many years. "Christine has to rely on herself. She does not need you two rutting dogs fighting over her."

Erik turned his head to gaze up at her and arched one black brow. "Rutting dogs, Madame?"

Madame Giry smiled and walked away. "Even Madame can lighten the moment at times, *oui*?"

After Madame had left, Erik remained alone. An astonished smile grew on his face as it struck him anew. "She came."

That night as Erik walked the streets of Paris toward his home, mindful that he was a hunted man, he chose the filthiest streets, littered with trash and the lowest forms of civilization. Though everything about his person bespoke wealth, from the cut of his fine clothing, to the highly polished onyx cane he carried, not one thief, not one prostitute dared approach. It took only a glance at this masked devil to warn anyone following that he or she invited danger by engaging him.

A few of the bolder prostitutes threw out lurid suggestions. Erik merely tipped his hat with overly dramatic flair and continued. His home lay near Madame Giry's, in a surprisingly reputable part of town. Erik reached his door and rapped twice with his cane. His butler opened the door immediately.

"Good evening, my lord." The butler took Erik's belongings.

"Good evening, Ducray. Please have a supper tray sent to my study. I will be spending most of my night there."

"Very good, my lord. I will see to it that your study is prepared." Ducray's voice contained as much starch as his immaculate uniform.

Erik loosened the stark white cravat from around his neck as he entered his study. He noted that the room had already been prepared in anticipation of his arrival. A snifter of brandy waited for his hand and several candles lighted his desk; the room had an ambiance of calm welcome, no doubt Ducray's handiwork.

"Prepare my study indeed, Ducray." The corner of Erik's mouth tugged upward. No matter how straight his butler's posture, how perfectly groomed his shock of white hair; the constant sparkle in those bright blue eyes always gave Erik a pause; Ducray appeared either to be having a laugh at his expense, or the entire world in general. Merriment was a relatively unknown concept to Erik, and he treated Ducray with a mixture of curiosity and reserve.

Erik picked up the brandy and cradled the snifter in his palm, registering its warmth within the glass. He settled behind a massive mahogany desk and gazed at the endless towers of books that surrounded him, their presence a comforting reminder of how he came to be here.

Four months before, Erik had become the Earl of Chester through a bizarre twist of fate. His mind traveled further back, touching on painful memories with hesitant probing.

He hadn't wanted to live after losing Christine. He submersed himself in his rage and self-loathing, until he stopped feeling anything at all. For weeks afterward, he existed on a plane not far from death, but not close enough. His world became a prison once again, this time a small, windowless room. Only through the bullying of Madame Giry did he finally resurface…through her bullying and one single memory: Christine's kiss. His heart latched onto that memory, and it dragged his will back from the abyss of purgatory he had wanted to plunge into.

Even when he learned of Christine and Raoul's swift marriage, he did not let himself slide back toward that precipice. Instead, he forced himself to relive the vicious killings he had committed, and decided he had no other option but to turn himself over to the mercy of the court.

He remembered the weight of Madame Giry's calm, assessing stare as he lay in his bed, empty of feeling, overflowing with memories. When she spoke, the emotion behind her steady words shook him.

"Sometimes, one must be broken in order to be fixed, Monsieur. To have come this far in your recovery only to decide you should hang? Because that *is* what will happen. You will never receive mercy from anyone when you do not believe, yourself, that you deserve it."

He knew she spoke the truth. But after existing behind his mask for so long, he did not think a person worth saving dwelled underneath. Perhaps all his behavior in the past was the sum of himself as an Opera Ghost and as a man. Still, this ballet instructor who hid her kind heart beneath a stiff façade saw something worthwhile, and Erik ached to know if her eyes indeed saw the truth of him.

As if she could read his mind, Madame added briskly, "I did not spend these last weeks saving you from death for lack of something to do." She turned away from him and rearranged a perfect vase of flowers on the dresser. "I am not saying because of the cruel and sheltered life you have led that I condone the murders. But that drunken stagehand—a lecherous swine! I lost track of how many of my girls he terrorized, that I saved from his unwanted advances! If he had gotten his filthy hands on my Meg..."

She clenched her fist around a fragile blossom, and then released it swiftly when she saw the damage she had wrought. "And the Prima Donna's lover? In your feverish ramblings, you apologized over and over, begging him to understand it was an accident. What happened that night?" Madame Giry threw the question out as if it burned her mouth and kept her gaze trained on the flower arrangement.

Moments passed, each second a suspended eternity until Erik at last spoke.

"It was an accident. But death does not care about such incidentals."

Even now, sitting in this library, years and experiences away from that day, Erik recalled how tight his throat had felt as he struggled to confess his horrible tale.

"I wound the rope around his throat, intending to render him unconscious—to have him out of my way—so that I could just get to Christine. I had to get to Christine! In truth, I had no idea the fool had died until I heard the cry. And still, I only thought of her...only cared about her. Accident or no, their deaths stain my hands."

Madame had continued to stare into the blooms and then at last turned to look at him. "I have seen evil men, Monsieur, men who truly have no soul and have all things handed to them on a silver platter from birth to death and continue to mete out hatred and violence. That is not who you are. You have so much to offer the world, so much to teach. If you truly feel remorse, then go... far away. Nurture the flame of your dark soul that Christine has lit. And if you return as the same man, then I will hang you myself!" She left him alone with her words and time to think on them.

In the end, Madame Giry had her way. Erik had been in no condition to fight her, but more than that, he wanted to believe her.

So he traveled to the furthest reaches of the world. He learned of different religions. He fed his need for culture. He filled himself with music. He found that a man did exist underneath the mask, and that he was a human being, worthy of more than his own violence suggested.

Fate agreed. In India he met Lord Sinclair, Earl of Chester, an old man who had little time left on this earth, a man without family or friends. In fact, very few things divided the Earl and Erik, for the Earl's face was disfigured as well.

Astonishingly, from that first meeting, Erik trusted Lord Sinclair, and refrained from sharing only two incidents in his past: his life before the opera and Christine. The familiarity was a first in Erik's life, and each day he feared he would lose this friend, this mentor. From that fear came times he deliberately sought the Earl's revulsion only to be met with empathy. Nothing Erik could say made the Earl turn his back on him.

"I consider myself a good man. And I believe that good men deserve to be happy and prosper. Sometimes it is not who we are that make us behave in certain ways. Sometimes it is our circumstances that dictate our actions." The Earl looked steadily into Erik's eyes. "We are both survivors of our different worlds. And I am telling you that you deserve to be happy and prosper."

Lord Sinclair also wore a mask. In fact, like Erik, he had several. He joked about their different names. "*The Dinner Mask*," the "*Earl Mask*," the "*I'm Weary, Leave Me Be Mask*." Lord Sinclair laughed at the people around them, silly people whose narrow minds recoiled from imperfection.

Erik began to understand what it meant to be whole.

One day not far into their acquaintance, the old Earl removed his mask in front of Erik.

"I wear these masks for them," he said, gesturing to the world, "not for myself. I am comfortable with who I am."

He did not look at Erik to follow suit, yet Erik wanted nothing more than to do so. Something broke free inside of him, like manacles ripped from their moorings. Heart pounding, he pulled the molded covering from his face. Erik was unmasked of his own free will for the first time in his life in front of another human being. And from that point on Erik and the Earl went without masks in the company of each other.

As Erik continued to grow and learn from this astonishing friendship, so came times that he would completely forget he did not wear a mask.

Chapter Four

ONE night, while in Russia, they attended an opera, "*Romeo and Juliet*", the tragic tale of ill-fated lovers. Erik listened with everything inside of himself. Tears fell unheeded down his cheeks. That night he told his companion of Christine.

Thoughtful, the Earl asked, "And what do you plan to do about her?"

Erik glared. "Do? Nothing! She has made her choice."

The Earl smiled. "My son, if this tale of yours is to be believed, then I have to think it is not finished."

"It is finished. She made that clear when she came back to give me this." Erik withdrew a ring from underneath his shirt. It hung from a chain around his neck.

The earl chuckled. "You wear the ring, yet it is finished."

Incensed at his friend's laughter, Erik snapped the chain and threw it on the table between them. "You mock me!"

The Earl picked up the ring and examined it carelessly. "What was it you told me about the first time you saw this bauble?"

Erik's face burned with embarrassment as he recalled the white-hot fury that had gripped him when he saw Christine wearing the ring as he did now. He recalled how he ripped it off of her neck, telling her she belonged to him! She belonged to him…A look of realization mixed with disbelief crossed his face.

"I am just an old man, but perhaps she was telling you something a little deeper." Lord Sinclair handed the ring back to Erik. "We will go to the jewelers in the morning. If you insist on removing jewelry in such a manner, order a much sturdier clasp."

As the Earl lay sleeping in the room next to his, Erik stood and stared out of his window until the sun reemerged along with his dreams.

Ironically their last outing together was the most painful. They had just arrived in Ireland when the Earl caught wind of a gypsy fair, another event on his list of things to experience before he died. Erik, unable to speak of his upbringing, joined him with vast reluctance. Only for the Earl would he revisit the horror of his youth.

As if his past recreated its abhorrent self, the sights, the smells, the brittle loudness of it all, everything about this life sickened Erik. In contrast, the Earl delighted in the gypsy adventure. He flirted and danced around a campfire with the gypsy girls. Had his fortune read by the old crone. Stuffed himself full of exotic delicacies. And through it all Erik remained silent. Finally, the end was in sight, the Earl declared he was satisfied. Then he spotted a small group of tents.

"We almost missed seeing our relatives, my boy!"

Side by side they approached the freak show. Erik's mind whimpered in protest, his soul recoiled with each step. Still, Erik could not stop, God help him, could not stop walking closer and closer to everything he loathed about himself.

A toothless gypsy woman stood outside the entrance to the tents. Her shrill voice called out to the crowds, "See the freaks! See the damned souls who God has punished!" She spotted the two masked gentlemen coming her way.

"Come right in gents, no need for masks. There's no shame in wanting to see the Devil's handiwork!" She grabbed at Erik's mask and pulled it off. At the sight of his face, she cackled. "Oho, escaped one of the cages did you, luv."

The crowd laughed and pointed at Erik. He froze in place, unable to move as jeering faces swam in and out of his vision. Through his haze he saw a filthy young gypsy boy grab at the Earl's mask.

"Another freak! Another freak!" The crowd's malicious attention shifted to this weaker prey.

Erik snapped out of his stupor. He grabbed the toothless woman by her throat.

"It is you who are the freak!" He threw her down. Taking his cane, he brandished it on the crowd with great force, until he reached his friend. The Earl lay on the ground, breathing hard, his clothes in disarray and his mask crumpled beside him.

Erik knelt down. "Are you all right?"

"...just need to catch my breath." Erik helped the Earl to a sitting position then reached over and gently placed the discarded mask in his friend's hand. Then he stood and faced the crowd.

"Have you all gorged yourselves enough? Is this what you needed to see?" He jumped at the crowd, a fearsome gargoyle, relishing their fear. "Every one of you here is a monster! A freak of nature! What kind of low creature would delight in seeing another's misfortune? What depraved soul would attack a gentle old man?" He swung his cane at them, indifferent to any injury he might inflict.

"Get out of here! Go home and see if you can look at yourselves in the mirror. I am disgusted by you. Do you understand? *I* am disgusted by *you*!" He turned back to his friend with absolute disregard to the people behind him.

And when he picked the Earl up and carried him back to their lodgings, he did not stop to retrieve his own mask. It lay in the dirt, unimportant.

After settling his friend in, Erik at last shared the story of his youth.

Tears filled the old man's eyes as he grasped Erik's strong hand within his frail ones. "I know that was very difficult, Erik, and I thank you for trusting me. I do believe God actually smiled down on me when he sent you into my life. I am proud to have been part of this journey with you. You deserve happiness—believe that my friend."

The Earl died in his sleep that night. Erik blamed the shock of the night's events for bringing death to the old man's bedside sooner than later.

A shock of different a nature followed shortly thereafter. The

Earl's solicitor informed Erik that his friend had bequeathed his title, his lands and all his holdings to Erik's name. With the flourish of a pen, the Opera Ghost had become one of the wealthiest men in Europe with one of the oldest titles.

―

Lord Sinclair, Earl of Chester, was buried in a family plot on his country estate in England. The ceremony consisted of Erik and the Earl's staff. It maddened Erik that this extraordinary man who had so much to offer the world was mourned by so few. He found the letter later that day.

> *My Son,*
> *For that is what you have become to me. I know that you found this letter in the bag that you are packing right now. Ducray honored my wishes that I have the last word with you. Even in death, I reserve the right.*
> *I want you to stop packing immediately. Sit down and think about what I have given you. Think about what it could mean. It is time to stop running.*
> *The papers will not be notified of my death, so you can make a smooth transition into your new role as the Earl of Chester. I have no family to contest my will. If anyone should pry, you are my illegitimate son whom I chose to acknowledge and I have provided the papers to prove it. I was quite pleased with myself for having come up with that. As for Ducray and the rest of my staff, they are completely trustworthy; you have nothing to fear in that direction. On second thought, keep an eye on that rascal Ducray; he has a penchant for the silver.*
> *I have given much thought to your Christine. Follow it through my friend. If I might suggest, put on my "Romance Mask" and go find her.*

With a quirk of his lips, Erik brought to mind the outlandish piece the Earl referred to: a half mask, pink, with delicate hearts and flowers painted around the eyes. He shook his head at his friend's fondness for the absurd and continued to read:

Above all, be careful. Many people in this world will never forget nor forgive. Thank you, Erik, thank you for being this old Earl's friend. I have learned so much from you in these past months. I love you.

Your friend,
Lord Thomas Sinclair

Erik gripped the letter and let the grief overtake him. Sobs rolled through his body in shuddering waves. He stayed for hours in his room, clutching the proof that someone had loved him. He had found redemption in the one thing he never expected to have in his desolate life. Friendship.

The man had finally moved out from behind the mask. The strange and comforting thing about this catharsis—he had purged the Opera Ghost, but could still feel the Phantom alive and well within him. And now it was time to let the Phantom play. Erik grabbed a piece of parchment and began to write.

Chapter Five

ONE, two, three, four...Christine sat in front of her vanity and pulled the pins from her hair with trembling fingers. The ride home with Raoul had been an ordeal. He looked so upset when he asked her if she had found what she was looking for, then became angry when he received no answers.

"You realize that this is a *man* who murdered innocent people? This creature whom you are seeking is a soulless beast who wants nothing more than to imprison you for his own pleasure, no matter what your feelings are. I thought I saved you from all this, but it would seem that I can't save you from yourself." Raoul threw himself back into the seat, his light blue eyes boring into her.

Words of self-recrimination had rushed to Christine's lips but went no further. The harsh truth for her to acknowledge was that she did want to see Erik. A monster that had killed, a creature that had terrorized...a man who possessed such vast amounts of sadness and beauty. She looked over at her husband's handsome face, so hurt and withdrawn, and suddenly wondered what in heaven's name she was thinking, running off to Madame Giry's in search of a Phantom. She would not do this to her innocent husband; she would not make him pay for loving her.

Christine reached to take his hand, tugged on it to have him look at her.

"Raoul, I should not have lied to you. Please...I will forget this madness as you say. I do love you."

They came to a stop in front of their home. Raoul stayed silent until he helped Christine descend the steps of the carriage. "If you do not keep your word, Christine, then God save us both. For I will kill the blackguard should I see him, or die trying." He stalked toward the front doors, and then stopped. "And if I am lucky enough to have the Phantom at the end of my sword, this time, your pleading will fall upon deaf ears!"

Christine could only watch her husband walk away.

A knock on the door interrupted her distressed recollections. Raoul waited outside, uncertain.

"May I come in?"

"Yes, of course. I-I was just taking my hair down. It sits so heavy all piled up."

Raoul smiled. "And I see Little Lotte has once again taken matters into her own hands instead of using her personal maid."

"Raoul, I am trying to become accustomed to letting others attend me. But at times I find it practical to do for myself."

He crossed her bedchamber to stand behind her. Their eyes met in the reflection of the mirror. He ran his fingers lightly through her long hair.

"I know this new life has been difficult on you. I had hoped that things would be a bit smoother. The Phantom certainly knows when to time his entrance." His rueful chuckle had a bite to it. "That is why I believe this will be good for you; a messenger just brought it by." Raoul tossed an invitation down in front of her. The address read, *to Miss Christine Daae*. The waxy, red seal had been broken.

Christine picked it up and looked at Raoul questioningly. "You opened this?"

"Yes." Raoul put his hands up in mock appeal. "It was for your own safety. I thought it strange that it was addressed to your maiden name."

Irritation rippled through Christine "I am not some child who needs protection, Raoul."

Raoul paid no heed to her comment and gestured eagerly to the card. "Please, read this Christine… I think this is exactly what you need."

Exasperated with Raoul's lack of sensitivity, Christine snatched up the card. She soon forgot her annoyance with Raoul as she read the startling missive.

> *Miss Daae,*
>
> *Forgive the late intrusion of this seemingly arbitrary note. I have been searching for you, the daughter of Gustof Daae, for quite some time. In my excitement of having found you, I extend this invitation to have luncheon with me tomorrow. I have been a great admirer of your father's work for many years. It gives me great pleasure to ask for your aid in the opening of the École de musique Gustof-Daaé. It is my fondest wish that you join me.*
>
> *Your Obedient Servant,*
> *Lord Sinclair, Earl of Chester*

Christine placed the card on the dressing table. "Earl of Chester? Do you know him?"

"I vaguely know the title. It's very English. He sounds like a lonely old man." Raoul pulled Christine up and kissed her chastely on the lips. "I think it's a fine idea, a school of music in honor of your father. In fact, I wish I had thought of it."

Christine turned wistful. "Yes, it is a fine idea. Father would have loved that, a school of music." She scanned the letter for the time and direction. "I'm to meet him at one o'clock. Would you like to come with me?"

Raoul shook his head regretfully. "I have several things to take care of here. Besides, it would be cruel of me to deny an old man the pleasure of your company alone."

Late that morning Christine prepared to leave, escorted by her personal maid and a footman. Raoul had arranged to send the man along as a precautionary measure for protection. While Christine understood Raoul's sentiment, it made her feel insignificant that he hadn't spoken with her first. Christine met the two outside and began walking down the steps to the awaiting post chaise. As they were climbing inside, she heard her name called.

Christine looked up, startled as Raoul hurried toward her. He caught up to her quickly and smiled. "I rearranged my schedule so that I could accompany you myself."

"Raoul, that's wonderful! In truth I felt a little odd going without you."

"Just let me retrieve my coat and we'll be off." Raoul headed back to the house.

Christine peered into the carriage. "Well it looks like you two have an unexpected holiday. My husband will accompany me." She smiled conspiratorially. "I would make the most of it." The footman gave Simone a lascivious wink to which she responded by giggling. They scampered with much speed out of the carriage.

When her husband did not return, Christine hurried back up the steps only to encounter him in the foyer, clearly agitated.

"Christine, I'm afraid I cannot accompany you after all. One of my tenants just arrived and is requesting an audience with me. Apparently there is some dispute over livestock ownership."

Disappointed, Christine asked, "Would you like me to wait?"

Raoul sighed. "No, I have no idea how long this will take. Most likely I will have to ride out and hear the other side of the story."

"I will miss you."

He kissed her cheek. "As will I."

It wasn't until Christine went back outside that she remembered that she had no escort. So she went alone.

Chapter Six

THE gothic church sat on the outskirts of Paris. Christine stood in front of the building, admiring the stonework and stained glass windows, an inspiring combination of rough strength and piercing beauty. Most would find it daunting, but Christine could not wait to discover what riches lay in store.

She pushed open one of the heavy, wooden doors, surprised to find it well oiled.

"Lord Sinclair? Hello?" Then, Christine forgot all else as she stepped into another world, her world.

The church was structured in the Latin cross style, the arched ceilings ornamented with plaster moldings of classical Greek inspiration, which reached so far upward Christine had to crane her neck. The pews had been removed to leave the floor wide open. Various crates now occupied the space and some lay opened, displaying hand crafted instruments from all over the world. Christine saw a desk piled high with sheets of music. A large stage rose to the left where singers could perform.

Another room that previously served as a chapel had been set up with dancer's "barres". Mirrors already lined the walls. The sun shone through the panes of the stained glass windows casting prisms of color everywhere. Breathtaking and inspiring, two perfect words floated through Christine's mind. "…music's throne…"

A slight flicker caught her eye. Only a few feet away, a shallow ledge carved its place in the stone wall. On the ledge, a single candle burned in front of a plaque. Christine stepped closer and inhaled with disbelief on recognizing the daguerreotype of her father that she had left behind in the Chapel of the Opera House. A sense of fate overtook her. Lovingly she traced her finger over his image, imagining she heard once again the beloved strains of his violin.

"Father, how you would have loved this place."

A delicate melody drifted to her ears. Christine inclined her head, listening intently. She ventured farther into the church, trying to locate the source and noticed a staircase that led up to one of the towers. The closer she walked, the clearer the sound became. Up, up she went following the music, so simple in its nature, so much more compelling for it. She had almost reached the top, when she heard *his* voice.

"If I held your hand in mine, and allowed myself a dream
The veils would be lifted, you would believe,
I am all that I seem."

The words were untainted emotion. Christine's heart trembled from the impact.

She reached the landing of the tower; his back was to her as he played his pipe organ. Softly enough to wonder if she imagined it, she heard. "Christine, please forgive me."

Another few steps brought her within inches of him. He continued to play without glancing at her.

"Silently I'll wait, while your heart decides my fate.
The monster's gone, this man's before you now,
Hoping we can move beyond the past somehow."

When he completed the last sweet chord, he sat unmoving, his dark head bowed toward the keys. Christine placed her fingertips upon his back, her vocal chords unable to function.

At her touch Erik exhaled harshly; in a flash of movement he was facing her.

"What do you see Christine?" His soulful emerald eyes seemed to command and plead.

She saw…everything. Still nothing came to her lips, which made no difference. No words would suffice to describe the emotions that raced though her body at the sight of her Phantom in all his glory. Half his features molded under the pure white mask, the rest of his sensual face carved by archangels. The air around him seemed to pulse with the force of his personality.

Mouth dry, she whispered, "My Angel…"

"No!" A stark denial. Christine almost wept at his tangible disappointment.

"No, Christine, I am not your Angel, I am not the spirit of your Father, I am not the Opera Ghost." He prowled the room, coming full circle to stand before her once again. "I am a man, merely a man."

Christine almost laughed at that statement. "Merely" was not a word to describe anything about him. He wished her to see him as a man? Did he not realize that if she did so, she would be without her armor? That if she looked into his exquisitely complex soul and acknowledged that the monster was indeed gone, she would be lost?

"Why have you come back?" The words pushed out, creating a distance between them.

Erik cocked his head, a devilish glint in his eye. "To win the heart of my fair Christine."

"You know that is impossible."

Erik only looked perplexed at her declaration.

"My apologies, you are correct." He paused as if considering something of enormous importance. "I meant to say, to win the heart, the mind, *and* the soul of my fair Christine."

He held her hand and placed a burning kiss on the tender skin of her palm, then closed her fingers around it.

Christine watched him, mesmerized by the impression of his lips that branded her skin. *What was she doing?* She snatched her hand back. Erik's keen gaze missed nothing, which increased her ire further.

"You have made a mistake. This meeting was a mistake. I am going home to my husband."

Erik's stance became rigid, his face darkened with each drawn breath. *Good,* she thought miserably, *I have made my point.*

As Christine turned to leave, his voice pierced through her sense of victory. "Yes, Little Lotte wouldn't want to upset her childhood sweetheart." Sarcasm barbed his words.

She stopped. "What is that supposed to mean?"

Erik approached her with predatory steps. "It means that he sees you as a child." When he reached Christine, he leisurely slid his finger down the length of her cloak, pushing it open to reveal her pastel yellow dress. "He dresses you as a virginal young girl." Christine slapped his hand away from her cloak. Erik chuckled and grabbed a hold of the golden locket around her neck. Christine shivered from the warm brush of his hand. They both remembered a similar circumstance, a similar rush of emotion. He flicked his gaze upward and locked eyes with her before releasing the locket with amused indifference. "A child's trinket."

His taunts had struck a nerve. "Raoul is all that is affectionate and caring!"

Erik's eyes kindled further at Raoul's name. He backed Christine up against the rough stones of the wall. Her eyes widened in alarm and…excitement. *Dear God, the excitement of Erik.*

He braced his large hands on the wall, over Christine's shoulders. She could slide down and out of this mock imprisonment if she chose.

"All that is affectionate and caring?" Erik repeated the words, making them sound empty as her heart felt when she uttered the declaration. He stood close. So close that the heat of their bodies merged and entwined. Then Erik leaned his head down; his lips poised by the sensitive curve of her ear—a breath away. "I *burn* for you, Christine."

The impassioned words wound their way inside of her and ignited something Christine experienced only one other time in her life. A stage. A song. A seduction. Christine wanted this fire. Wanted to plunge into the scorching flames and fuse her entire being with this man. This man who was not her husband. Shame rose up inside her and she shoved Erik away. He stumbled back, never taking his eyes from her face, watching as one would watch a startled doe.

"You are the only one who affects every part of who I am." This came out as an accusation. "I have to leave." Christine angrily brushed away betraying tears.

Erik kept his voice gentle, belying the fierce elation that shone in his eyes. "Christine. Wait."

Christine shook her head. "No, this is wrong! Why can't you see that?"

"Christine." Erik used the pad of his thumb to wipe a falling teardrop. "Stay with me...stay with me and enjoy this repast I have arranged." He motioned to a table Christine had not noticed before, set with china as delicate as any the de Chagny family possessed.

She hardened her resolve. This was insanity. "You are a killer."

"No. I have killed. I have only known parts of myself. My music, my love for you, my fury, these were all things that made my existence real. I did not realize that the monster lived all the way down in the furthest reaches of my soul, that to keep you I would become a crazed being capable of murder."

Christine could see the remorse and disgust in his eyes as he continued to speak. "Murder, my definition of survival. I have laid myself bare to my own scrutiny and found myself worthless. It wasn't until I met a great man that I was able to see myself clearly and understand the changes I needed to make. If it hadn't been for you, Christine I never would have had the courage to trust in another human being or the courage to believe that I had any worth."

Almost undone before such honesty, Christine knew she should turn around and walk away. It was such a simple thing to do. It was impossible. Again, she tried to fight his pull. "You say you are different, yet you still hide behind your mask."

Erik touched the mask absently. "Ah yes, the mask. I wear the mask...for them." He gestured vaguely to the world outside.

Christine wondered what recollection brought such a fond smile to this inscrutable man. Her mind trod on dangerous territory as she began to question what changes *had* been wrought within Erik.

How had they come about? *Turn and walk away, just walk away before it's too late.*

Erik pounced, as if he sensed her weakening resolve. "Please, Christine. A brief moment of your time, that's all I ask of you."

But he asked so much more, and both were aware of it.

Christine could no longer deny herself what she truly wanted—a chance to know the man who had never stopped living inside her mind.

"Am I to dine with Erik or the Phantom?"

"We are one and the same, I'm afraid." Then, with all the vulnerability of the world showing in his soulful eyes, Erik took Christine's hand into his own. He guided it up to the white mask. Could not seem to breathe as her fingers curled around the edges and pulled it gently away from his face.

She put the mask down onto the pipe organ. "Am I not one of them?"

"No. You never have been. I allowed my own revulsion to deform my soul and my sight. I could not see past that to anyone, especially you, who might behold me otherwise."

"Thank you," Christine breathed. "Thank you for telling me this."

She let Erik guide her to the table, noted the perfect red rose in its crystal vase and listened to his tale.

Hours later they whispered tender good-byes as dusk covered the city of Paris. Christine had promised to meet him the following morning, and Erik was content to leave it at that. Something monumental had shifted between them. Erik had sensed a softening; he knew she wanted to believe in him. She would be here again tomorrow. Tomorrow had never held such promise.

Erik waited until the carriage disappeared from his sight and walked back into the school. He held onto the memory of her long ago kiss. Held onto the hope that in the end, she could love him.

Raoul was not home when Christine arrived. Simone informed

her that he had been out all day and wouldn't return until the following evening. Too relieved to question his whereabouts, Christine went straight to bed that night and dreamt of music.

Chapter Seven

A SMALL envelope awaited Christine when she arrived at Erik's school the next day. He had placed it in front of the plaque of her father, along with a red rose. She smiled at her father's image.

"He still knows me so well." She lit her candle and began to open the envelope.

"You are not allowed to read that yet."

Christine spun around to find Erik standing in a ray of sunlight, without his mask.

He held out his hand for the envelope.

She gave it to him and looked at him quizzically. "Then why leave it there for me to find?"

Erik smiled, and for the blink of an eye Christine saw a mischievous boy. "It is the Phantom in me. Let us see how our morning progresses. Then I will decide whether to give you the envelope or not. Come, let me show you the school." He took her hand, but Christine stood where she was.

"You left your mask off." With the greatest care she reached up and ran her fingertips down the ravaged side of his face.

"You know all that I am. I will never hide from you again."

"What if I don't know all that I am?"

"Then that would be a devastating loss for both of us." Trepidation kept him from explaining his remark. How could he say that if she didn't know herself, there was no chance of her returning to him? He could see that Christine's soul was adrift, her music lost to her. *What had becoming the Vicomtesse done to her, his glorious Christine?*

Erik ignored the sense of foreboding that shadowed his heart. He would have his Christine back. Once again he would be playing the Devil to Raoul's Angel, but this time the Devil would save her soul.

"Christine, I would like it if you assisted me in making a success of this school."

Christine lowered her head, but not before Erik discerned her sorrow. Face still averted, she pleaded, "Please don't put this dream in front of me when I cannot live it. I would have to lie to my husband every day that I spent here with you."

Then leave that pretentious whelp. "Of course, I was wrong to ask that of you." Erik felt no remorse for playing on Christine's guilt. "But I still must live in the shadows, and this school dedicated to your father should not have to suffer the same fate."

Christine's eyes rested on her father's plaque. The flame of the candle flared brighter. Erik followed her stare and saw the wonder in her eyes.

Deeper into the building he led her, until they stood in the middle of the marble floor. He strode a few feet away and swept out his hand. "This is our world Christine. We were created for music. To deny yourself that would be a travesty." His fervent words echoed throughout the walls.

He cupped Christine's face with his hands, his eyes traveled ardently over every nuance of his beloved's features. "Do you remember, Christine?" Erik softened his midnight voice to a lover's whisper, delicate as the brush of an angel's wing.

Christine put her small hands over his, her eyes moist. Wisps of melody danced about in her memories, pale copies of the rich sound that used to play there.

"Christine, close your eyes," came the velvet command.

She did so without thinking, the slight tremble of Erik's hands underneath her own sent a wave of tender awareness through her—he was as nervous as she!

"Please sing for me, Christine."

Her eyes flew open. "S-sing for you?" Christine's face warmed in embarrassment. "Oh."

"Christine?"

Erik's hard stare rooted her to the spot when she wanted nothing more than to flee. In mortification she watched his expression change from startled bemusement to smoldering perception. "I misunderstood, Erik. Please stop looking at me like that." Christine tried to distance herself from his probing eyes and her rampant longing. "The moment has passed, Erik. It is over."

"The moment has not yet begun Christine," his gravelly voice answered, and he pulled her to him in one fluid motion.

Erik's lips hovered over hers; his eyes demanded that she make up her mind now, this instant. Christine understood he gave her one final chance to change her mind.

Her heart thudded. His music still played in her thoughts. Her soul thrilled in expectation. *Yes*, she responded in thought, while her mouth had already fused to his.

The kiss was primitive. A melding of two souls created before Adam and Eve, before time, destined to each other. *At last, at last*, their hearts murmured as the kiss deepened. The music inside Christine grew into a crescendo. Tears began to flow down her cheeks and dampened Erik's. He placed his lips on each of her tears and then held her. He held her while her soul came back to life.

As she clung to Erik, Christine longed to live in this perfect instant. But wishes did not come true, nor did they change her reality. The last strains of song faded from her mind.

With great reluctance she broke away from Erik's strength. "I need to think about this and…that is all I can give you right now."

She knew it cost him, yet Erik gave an abbreviated nod, and before she walked out the door, he slipped the envelope into her hand.

Guilt made its bleak appearance on the drive home. It weighed Christine down. She labeled herself a vile human being. She had betrayed Raoul and her own morals. It was to her greater shame and confusion that she could not wait to reach her home to see what Erik had written.

Immediately upon arrival, Christine went straight to her chambers. She locked the door, ripped open the envelope and found a poem.

> *I would like to venture softly into your soul*
> *And be absorbed by the colors*
> *I would like to wander amongst your fantasies*
> *And fulfill every one*
>
> *I would like to touch you from the inside out*
> *And know you so deeply*
> *I would love to journey into your heart*
> *And find myself there*
>
> *Your Obedient Servant,*
> *Erik*

After reading it several times, Christine hid the wondrous verse inside her box of stationery.

Her worst desire had been realized. Erik had become the person that she had always known lived inside of him. He had merged the genius of his Phantom with his poet's heart. He had restored the radiant soul that had been damaged so many years ago. It had been so easy to pity him, to fear him, knowing that she would never have to worry about losing her heart to a deranged madman. During the day's conversations, she searched desperately for any signs of the same creature she had run from. All she found was Erik. A potent ambrosia of passionate intensity, tempered now with calmness, a sense of self he hadn't had before.

She thought of Raoul. His love had been a sweet balm compared to her Angel's harsh possessiveness. Raoul had provided peace whereas the Angel threatened horror.

But the Angel was no more. Erik's love demanded, seduced, and it also worshipped and gave. Christine felt as if she'd rediscovered herself this afternoon in his presence. He let her see herself through his eyes, holding nothing back. She remembered the music, remembered her talent, the feel of her voice joined with his, soaring so high! Erik, Erik…it was happening again. Her soul had awakened and stretched its wings, ready to take flight alongside him. Black remorse clashed with the bright stirrings of new love. *Raoul*, she thought despairingly, *am I already lost to you?*

Chapter Eight

DINNER was a strained affair. Distracted and tense, Raoul would look up from his plate now and then as if he had something to say. Each time he chose not to speak, the tension became more palpable. The past two days had created an invisible gulf. Christine could stand it no longer.

"Raoul, what is it?"

Once more, he started to speak and then decided against it. "I have many things on my mind. I'm not a very good company this evening, I'm afraid. I trust that your elderly companion provided more entertainment?"

Christine's surroundings became surreal. Did he know? Was he baiting her? She plucked her glass of red wine from the table and took a deep sip.

"He was not what I expected."

Christine saw him visibly relax.

"So, he was older and more feeble than we had thought?" Raoul asked.

Now she experienced a tightening of nerves at the new direction into which the conversation had veered. She cut into her roasted pheasant with great precision, avoiding Raoul's eyes. In her uneasy state, she rambled carelessly. "Well, yes he is older. His mind however, is nothing short of brilliant. A true connoisseur of music."

"I've never heard you so impressed with someone, Christine. He must have loved you." Raoul looked pleased with the thought.

A tiny bite of pheasant lodged in her throat. She needed more wine to wash it down. Christine took a healthy swallow from her glass and it did nothing at all to alleviate the constricted feeling. Now that she knew Raoul had no idea as to the true identity of the Earl, she felt like she was playing him for a fool.

Truly nauseated, Christine excused herself. "I think I need some fresh air…do you mind?"

"What is it?" Raoul jumped up from his chair and helped Christine to her feet.

His concern only made her feel worse. I'm just a little tired." She gave him a small smile when he frowned. "Truly, it's nothing. I think I'll go for a walk in the gardens and then to bed."

Once in the gardens, Christine burst into tears. She had to stop this now. She did not know what cruel madness had taken hold of her senses and allowed her to envision a future with Erik. Raoul was her husband and deserved better than this from her, far better. Tomorrow she would pen Erik a note telling him how she felt.

She sank down on a stone bench. Luxuriant red roses surrounded her. Christine ignored the temptation to caress the petals and lose herself to their allure. Instead she gazed at them, letting her eyes feast on what she would not allow herself to touch.

"Christine, are you out here?" Raoul's voice broke through the quiet. He came around a path. "There you are. It seems I am forever trying to find where you have gone." He noticed her tears and sat down beside her. "Oh, Little Lotte…." Raoul gently held her hand. "May I ask you something?" At Christine's nod he continued. "It occurred to me that…though it's been some time…with you not feeling well and then these tears, perhaps you are…"

Softly, Christine cut him off. "I am not with child." She felt as if lifetimes had passed since she and Raoul first discussed starting a family.

"Oh, I see." Disappointment colored his tone. Raoul looked away for a moment. "There is something else I wanted to talk to you about. You might be angry with me, but it was my only option."

Alarm bells clanged in Christine's head. "What did you do Raoul?"

"I spoke with a police investigator yesterday, informing him that the Opera Ghost has returned. They started the manhunt today. That is why I haven't been at home."

Her first instinct was to slap Raoul's face. Her second was to protect Erik. Raoul must have read Christine's mind.

"Don't you dare try to protect him!" His voice became anguished. "Don't you dare." He reached out and plucked a rose off of a bush. He held it in his open palm, staring at it. "Do you know how it feels to watch someone you love slip away? To know that the love that once seemed so secure is crumbling before your eyes, destroyed by some fiend. I do. I know."

Slowly he tore a petal off of the rose, then another, and another. Christine watched in silence as the bloom was stripped bare of its beauty.

"Nothing has been the same since that night on the balcony. I will tell you something else, Christine. I did not have any meeting here in France. I left you alone in England because I became obsessed with the thought of proving the Opera Ghost's death to you. I went back to his lair for evidence of his demise."

Her mind reeled in shock. "You went back there? Oh, Raoul, you should have discussed this with me."

Raoul tossed the bud onto the ground and stared at Christine in astonishment. "I should have discussed this with *you*? Perhaps I did not do so because you had already chosen to withhold certain information from *me*, Christine. Perhaps, as I traveled downward and relived the horror of a noose wrapped around my neck while watching my fiancée place her chaste lips upon a grotesque demon, I wondered why my wife did not *discuss* a rose given to her on a balcony in the moonlight."

He had seen the rose? "Dear God, Raoul. I did not know what to do; I did not know what to say. Had I any notion that my actions would lead you back there…" Her tone beseeched him to understand. "I did not know."

"His lair is destroyed, but we both know that the Opera Ghost lives. I picked my way through broken glass, shredded papers, shattered bits of this and that, and did not find a damn thing to slake my most fervent thirst. He lives, and he has come back to reclaim what is his. And you are, Christine—you are his. I hoped that I could fill whatever void …but I see now—" Raoul's voice broke. "I love you so. Please, tell me I am mistaken."

Would her heart ever feel joy again? If Raoul had lashed out, if he had abused, she would have walked away. Could have walked away. Now she had no choice but to remain. Tomorrow she would write to Erik, and warn him. Tonight she would sleep in her husband's bed. She would be the perfect wife. She would not disappoint him again. Christine stroked Raoul's golden hair gently.

"Darling, I think that it's time," she had to pause, as a great sense of loss engulfed her, "I think that it's time we started our family."

Happiness and relief suffused his features. "A child is just what we need. It will be living, breathing proof of our love, our bond!"

If the idea that Christine made this decision for him alone had crossed his mind, he did not dwell on it. Raoul led his wife back to the house, treading on the rose petals as he walked while Christine carefully stepped around them.

Chapter 9

My Dear Lord Sinclair,

It is with deepest regret that I impart this news. I am unable to share in the creation of my father's school. I have many responsibilities at home and to my husband.

I hope that you understand and can forgive me. Please do not cease to build upon what you have started because of my choice. It would be a great loss to do so.

You have honored me and my father beyond words. I will never forget you for that.

One more thing, if you choose to spend time alone at the school, please exercise caution. There are those who would hunt an unknowing man down.

Always,
Christine de Chagny

"That is a bit dramatic don't you think?"

Christine felt ready to scream. Raoul had stood over her shoulder the entire time she penned her letter. She couldn't even have a last indulgence to say good-bye in her own words. Everything she wanted to write, all her feelings, all her sorrow, had to be coded from Raoul's watchful eyes. But the true travesty of it all was the fact that Erik's poem laid underneath the stationery she was writing on. The only way to keep Raoul from seeing the poem would be to hide it within the letter. Her heart wept at the injustice. Erik would never know it was unintentional. She could only pray that this did not destroy all that he had become.

Christine placed her hands flat against the vellum. The polite words burned into her palms. "He is a wonderful man. I want him to know how much his generosity means to me."

"Little Lotte, such a soft heart." He watched Christine slowly and carefully fold the letter and seal it inside the envelope. "You know, you could still assist him. Even if you become pregnant I don't see how it would interfere."

Pregnant with Raoul's child while working alongside Erik? Horrified laughter bubbled to the surface. Christine pushed it down with effort.

"My life is here Raoul. It has been hard enough trying to fit into your world. I do not need to add more fodder for the gossips. A woman who is breeding has no place in such an environment."

Raoul said nothing. Christine voiced his exact thoughts. Thoughts he kept to himself because they made him feel selfish. He wanted Christine to put her past life away and forget about it. Their social standing still deteriorated before his eyes. He needed to think of his family. Both of his sisters had vacated the house for an unplanned holiday, making it clear that they would only return upon Christine's departure. Raoul was tired of his role as understanding husband. Christine must start caring about her title and the importance it held. He picked up the letter.

"You are right, Christine, that would be improper. We need to make a break from the past, for good. I would suggest you sever all ties with Madame Giry as well. I need you to embrace your role as Vicomtesse de Chagny and forget about the chorus girl I ..." Raoul faltered, unsure what hidden thought had almost been voiced. "I'll have this letter delivered." He left the room abruptly.

The impact of his decree though unsurprising, stunned Christine. But the absolute knowledge of what he hadn't said crippled her. She sadly finished her husband's sentence to the empty room. "Forget about the chorus girl I fell in love with."

The sound of shattering glass came from the Earl of Chester's bedroom, followed by several crashes. Then silence. Erik stood amidst the shambles of his room, chest heaving, his emotions still seething for release. He heard a polite knock on his door and ignored it, looking wildly about for something else to smash. The knock sounded again. A growl issued from deep in his throat.

Erik wrenched open the door. "What is it?"

Ducray held out a remarkably ugly vase. "The master always hated this."

"And?" Erik's voice teemed with hostility.

"Perhaps you could see fit to destroy it if you have run out of stock in your room. I have no liking for it, either." Ducray waited as if he found nothing odd in the present situation.

Erik's nostrils flared as he took a deep breath. He glared at Ducray, incredulous at the audacity of the man.

Ducray raised his brows in innocent inquiry, "My lord?"

Erik grabbed the vase from Ducray and turned back to his room. He raised his arm to hurl it against the wall then caught his reflection in the jagged glass of a broken mirror. A distorted monster stared back. He recognized this creature all too well. Erik wrenched himself away from the reflection, the destruction he wreaked within himself disgusted him far more than any ruined furniture or broken glass. He began to calm in small degrees.

"Damn you, Ducray."

"As you wish, my lord."

Ducray strolled away with considerable dignity. Once out of sight, he stepped behind a large potted plant and stopped to listen. He smiled in relief when all was silent. Looking up to the heavens, he murmured, "I am keeping my word old friend. I will watch over him as best I can."

"Ducray." Erik stood in his doorway, a beaten warrior, but not a broken one.

Though startled, Ducray nevertheless placidly inquired. "Yes, My Lord?"

"Thank you."

"Yes, My lord." Ducray moved out from behind the plant and

resumed his duties.

Erik sorted Christine's letter from the shattered fragments on the floor. Anguish twisted him in its brutal grip. The formal words hadn't changed. Oh, he could read between the lines, could see her heartfelt apology for what it was. But the end result remained unchanged. Christine had once again rejected his love. Once again had chosen Raoul. If the letter had come alone he might still have hope, but when the poem fell out of the envelope and dropped to the floor, his heart had fallen along with it. Only this time it hadn't just been damaged. It had been destroyed.

Crouched on the floor, amongst the destruction, the note crushed in his fist, he whispered sadly into the empty room, "We were bound to each other. I gave you my heart. And now you've denied me, you've crushed me, and you've lied to me." Tears fought for release, but Erik would not let them fall.

He stood suddenly and reread the last line of her letter with a scornful eye. "You thought to save me from being arrested? How kind. But you are dealing with the Earl of Chester now. Spare me your empty concern, Vicomtesse."

After all, who would think to find the infamous Opera Ghost residing in a nobleman's home?

Erik threw the crumpled paper to the floor.

He hated her for her power of reducing him. He hated himself for giving that power to her. He hated the only woman he would ever love.

Erik strode from his room to his study on the floor below. He had plans to attend to. The Earl of Chester might never show his face, but money had a way of making a man well known.

Chapter Ten

"THIS is a work of art. You have done well, Monsieur." Madame Giry walked around the school, her normally severe features softened in appreciation.

Erik merely grunted in reply as he unpacked the last of the instruments. Madame Giry paid no notice to his lack of response. He had been uncommunicative for weeks now. The only thing he spoke of was the school, and she had reason to believe the only time he let himself experience any emotion was when he played his pipe organ.

One evening she had come up to the tower while he played, so immersed in his song that he did not hear her approach. Madame recalled how hard she had gripped the banister as tears welled up in her eyes. Erik's face contained so much pain and heartbreak. But for all the suffering that he revealed, the absence of hope caused her deep sadness, for she could see the broken young boy within the man.

Erik abruptly slammed his hands down on the keys with a discordant crash. "Please, go!"

Madame Giry left quietly and they had never spoken of it.

She looked over her list of applicants. "I will need an assistant. Running a school of this magnitude is not a job that can be done alone."

"Do whatever you see fit. After I finish here today, I will not be coming back." Erik walked over to the plaque of Gustof Daae. "There is no joy for me here." He snuffed out the flame of the candle with two fingers. "There is no joy for me at all."

After everything that she had been through with this man, Madame still felt as if she could not intrude into Erik's personal thoughts. The irony of the fact that she was just as unapproachable was not lost on her.

Madame decided to stick to the business at hand. She could not let Erik withdraw. Even if she weren't capable of showing empathy, she was unparalleled at issuing orders.

"That is not acceptable. I will need you here until I have hired some help."

Erik's remained implacable. "No."

"Monsieur, there is still much to be done. *Mon Dieu!* You ask too much of me."

"I could say the same, Madame." Erik surveyed the room; he couldn't help but feel a sense of accomplishment, though melancholy tinged his triumph. The school had become a true homage to music. It saddened him that once again, because of his past and his face, he would not be able to play an active part in his creation. He knew Madame Giry suspected that Christine affected this decision not to come back, but in truth, he could not bring himself to once again dwell in the underground while those above lived out his dreams.

Christine by his side would have made all the difference. To conceal himself in the shadows and watch, knowing he had her love, would have made it bearable, would have eased the ache.

"I will not be coming back," he repeated. The words came out clipped and hard. "That is my final word on the subject." He felt a driving need to escape from Madame Giry's shrewd gaze.

"Very well Monsieur. It would seem that the Earl of Chester's kind actions do not extend to friends, but only to strangers."

Erik picked up a sheet of music from a table and idly studied it. "You might as well continue, Madame. I am all that is attentive."

Madame Giry grabbed the sheet from him and slammed it down on the table. His black brows drew together, a portent of the coming storm.

Madame ignored his look. "You are trying to recreate your Opera Ghost and nothing good will come of it."

"I beg your pardon?"

"I may not be about in society, Monsieur, but I am not without my connections. The Earl of Chester's name is on everyone's lips. I have heard that the Earl is building an orphanage, that he donates large amounts of money to different charities, not to mention helping fund Paris's war department. And th-"

Erik cut her off. "I fail to see the parallel, Madame. My anonymous good deeds have no resemblance to the Opera Ghost's behavior. If that is all?" Erik retrieved his dark cape from a nearby coat stand.

Madame Giry watched him. "What about box number five?"

His expression shuttered, Erik picked up his cane. "What about it, Madame?" he asked impatiently.

"Your deeds are not all good, Monsieur. I have also heard the mysterious Earl has bought up the loans of several noblemen. In fact that is how you came to own box number five; I believe it belonged to Count de Valette. You now hold many powerful men in your debt. What is the purpose of all this?"

Erik picked up the last item of his belongings. He placed the white mask carefully over the damaged side of his face and fixed his sardonic gaze on Madame Giry. "I haven't the slightest idea, but I am without a doubt confident that it will be something beyond my wildest speculations."

Erik bowed to Madame, threw open the front doors, and blended in with the night.

Madame Giry's head throbbed. She wished that her daughter were there.

Always an observer of human nature, Meg had matured into an insightful woman, and she could use her daughter's insight now. Madame shut the doors with a solid click and locked them. Meg's ballet troupe was not so far away that she couldn't be reached. The thought soothed Madame's troubled spirit.

"You are setting the stage once again Monsieur Phantom. But for what?"

Chapter 11

CHRISTINE lived as a ghost in Raoul's world. With each ball, each musicale, each dinner they attended, she felt herself fade a little more. Every time someone deliberately ignored or consciously overlooked Christine, something withered inside her. She wished she could grant these lords and ladies their fondest wish, and become invisible so they could have their darling Vicomte back.

Tonight they attended another dinner party, a small affair of thirty or so people. Raoul pulled Christine aside before joining the other guests.

"Are you feeling all right, Christine?"

No, Raoul, I feel as if I am dying from the inside out.

"Yes, Raoul, I am fine. We have been going to so many parties that I'm most likely a bit fatigued."

Please, see how this is hurting me. Please, let me know that I am more important than all of this. Please, take me home and hold me.

Raoul looked concerned. "Are you...?"

Deflated, Christine shook her head. "No, I am not. Raoul, we have only been trying for a short time. Though I don't think agreeing to every invitation you receive is helping matters."

Christine flinched from the lash of anger in his eyes before his words struck her as well. "Really, Christine? And I do not think that your obvious disregard of my friends is helping either. Can you not be bothered to extend one civil word?"

She had not realized how grossly Raoul misjudged her

withdrawal.

Burning frustration crackled within each accusation he branded her with. "You keep yourself apart from everything and everyone. I thought you were going to try this time. Can't you see how important this is to me? If we don't fit in here, there is no place that the two of us can belong."

His voice took on an edge of panic, and it dawned on Christine that Raoul's callous attitude to her situation came from his frantic need to see it that way. He needed to think that acceptance could be had if she only would put her best foot forward. Fear of losing his place in his world caused Raoul to place the burden of success completely on Christine's shoulders.

Christine tried to present her argument in way that connected to his rational side. "Raoul, you and I both know that isn't the case. These people will not let me in. I want you to be happy...I want us to be happy. I don't know what else to do." *Isn't my love for you enough?*

"Try harder." He extended his arm to her. "It is almost time for dinner. Let us join the others. And please put a smile on your face. Even a false one will do."

Christine had become adept at her pasted-on smile. Indeed, it had become her mask. Arm in arm they glided into the drawing room.

Dinner took an immeasurably long time to complete. Raoul had been ensconced next to the fawning hostess, who had relegated Christine to the far end of the table. He gave her an apologetic look before hastening to his own seat. Several times throughout the courses she attempted eye contact, but Raoul was far too busy entertaining the people around him. They vied for his attention and sought his approval in contrast to the conversations that flowed over and through Christine. Though Raoul was blind to it, she could clearly see the monstrous wall erected between herself and these aristocrats. The question was: on which side did her husband stand?

After dinner, the ladies retired to the large salon while the men lingered over their port. The woman clustered around a fortepiano, choosing songs. Christine entered behind them and sat alone on a divan, wondering how much more of this evening she would be forced to endure.

The gentlemen finally arrived, and Christine's ears immediately picked up on their conversation. "…what do you know of the Earl of Chester?" she overheard.

A young man answered. "No one knows much about the fellow except that he has a fortune to spend."

"Well, he is putting his money where it is most needed. That earns him my respect," an older gentleman put in.

"Earl of Chester? Isn't that an English title? Why does he reside in Paris?"

This came from a petite, dewy-eyed, debutante who had been lingering near the doorway.

Christine noticed that Raoul bestowed a charming smile on the girl before responding. "Who wouldn't choose to live in Paris over England?"

Approving laughter met his remark.

Raoul looked over to Christine and she met his gaze, unable to veil her misery. She saw Raoul flush, then excuse himself from the men and cross the room to her. To her puzzlement, he bestowed a most apologetic smile on her and held out his hand. Raoul's abrupt mood changes were beginning to concern Christine, yet she couldn't bring herself to care overmuch. Caring took so much energy. She took his hand in her limp grasp and allowed him to pull her up next to him.

Raoul beamed at the roomful of people and drew Christine in front of him, his hand resting on her shoulder. "My wife has actually met this enigmatic Earl." All attention suddenly veered to Christine. "She has been assisting him with one of his many charitable projects." Embarrassed, Christine wanted to shrink away from her boastful husband.

Some of the guests looked at her with a curious light in their eyes. One woman questioned, "What project is that, Vicomtesse?"

Raoul smiled encouragingly at her, but he squeezed her shoulder once, in warning. Resentment heated Christine's blood.

He wanted her to dramatize her relationship with the Earl and keep her mouth shut regarding her origins.

In a deliberate voice she said. "The ***École de musique Gustof-Daaé,*** named after my father, a famous violinist."

With that clear reminder of who she was and what her background held, the women turned their backs to her and gave their attention once again to the fortepiano. The men struck up a hasty conversation. Raoul's face turned a blotchy red.

"I will not let you do this to me," he hissed under his breath. He grabbed Christine's arm, all but dragging her over to the ladies. "May I ask that my wife be the first to sing, as you heard she has been involved with music her entire life." He thrust Christine forward.

Christine stared at Raoul. "No, please..."

Raoul held his hand up to silence her. "Now, Christine. I think you should bestow the gift of your voice on my esteemed friends. After all, that is what made me fall in love with you again." His words contained honey while his eyes contained venom.

Their hostess held up several choices of music. "Will this be a duet, Vicomte?"

Christine glanced at her husband. *Don't do this to me, my love.*

He paid her no heed. "No." he said shortly. "A solo."

The hostess smiled maliciously as the Vicomte left his wife's side.

"I see." She then made a selection and questioned sweetly, "I will play for you then, Vicomtesse?"

Christine watched Raoul select a seat near the debutante he had flirted with earlier and forced herself to give a small nod. She felt so empty. Her husband's spiteful behavior stabbed at her and she could feel any vestiges of hope seep out from the wounds.

She stood next to the woman and studied the song. The ballad had been written as a duet. Christine would sound ridiculous singing by herself. The woman settled herself on a small bench and began to play, not bothering to hide her smirk. Christine looked at no one as she began to sing.

"A place for us someday we'll find
Where love is true and fates are kind
A place that I can lend my heart
True to him though torn apart"

Her flawless voice touched even the most jaded listener. Raoul now gazed at her with admiration. It did not matter. He did not understand how much this had cost her. Christine hadn't sung since their honeymoon, and hadn't truly opened her vocal chords since the last night in the Opera House; yet her voice remained true. Her voice, a gift from Erik, now caused her heart to overflow with him from the first note sung.

Christine drew strength from her father's memory as the music changed tempo prior to the duet. He would want her to be strong right now. She continued her song, pained to know that of the two men who sustained her in this trying situation, neither one was her husband. He sat apart from her, pleased with his wife's performance, uncaring of her feelings.

"No Chains to hold us
No Sorrows dwell
Our final release from this blessed hell"

She did not notice the small commotion in the back of the room until she saw the large, hooded figure swiftly approaching her. His mask was a black nightmare, a grotesque, leering devil. His voice was pure joy, worthy of any angel.

The Opera Ghost sang with her.

"A place for us beyond the storm"

He reached Christine in an instant and stared down at her, his eyes glittering dangerously behind the ebony mask.

Raoul could not move, transported to another time when he had watched these two sing together. Watched their souls strain toward each other. It would not happen again!

"A place without the tearing thorns
There is somewhere past right or wrong
A place where only we belong..."

Raoul jumped from his seat. "This fiend is the Opera Ghost!" He cursed when he realized he had no weapon. None of the men did. Someone tried to open the doors; they had all been locked. Pandemonium broke loose. Movement, shouts, her husband, these things became a blurred reality; close by, but unable to touch the vivid color, the fine details within the cocoon of Christine and Erik. They gazed at each other, attuned and silent, still locked in music's embrace.

"What are you doing here?" Christine asked breathlessly.

The spell that wove around the two dissolved instantly.

Erik sneered at her. "I did not come for you. That time is past."

He withdrew a long, deadly looking sword from under his cloak and whirled to face the roomful of people. They quieted at once. "Good evening, good Messieurs." The Opera Ghost faced the woman on the fortepiano and inclined his head courteously. "And Mesdames." She slid off of the bench in a dead faint. No one dared move to assist her.

"Christine!" Raoul's voice shook.

Christine's gaze flew to her husband's panicked visage, but she did not move.

The Opera Ghost left nothing to chance; he barred Christine from straying by using the flat of his blade to block her way.

"Tsk, tsk." He wagged a black-gloved finger playfully. "You are not going anywhere near the Vicomte until I am through with him."

One of the younger gentlemen inched toward a slightly opened window.

"Monsieur, kindly step away from that window as it is my escape route. Do not force me to bruise the delicate sensibilities of the young ladies present." The Opera Ghost waited, an unpleasant smile on his face, while the young man backed away. "My thanks. Now as for you." He pointed the sword directly at Raoul's heart as he advanced on him. The hood of his cloak framed the ghoulish mask, intensifying the Opera Ghost's menacing aura.

Christine held her fist against her mouth to keep from crying out. She feared more for Erik's well being than Raoul's. Whatever Erik was doing, instinct told her this was more about his own self-destruction than anyone else's.

The point of the sword came to a stop against Raoul's chest. The Opera Ghost pressed it forward for emphasis. "I could dispose of you right now and end this farce. Your pathetic hunt for me will never bear fruit." Raoul glared at the Opera Ghost and gave an involuntary wince as the blade pushed a fraction deeper, cutting through the crisp white fabric of his shirt. "Remember this night, Vicomte. I found you. I hunted *you* down." The Opera Ghost stepped back to Christine; he looked straight at Raoul as he held Christine's chin in a rough grasp.

"This you can keep."

He pushed her away, and with a flash of motion smoke filled the salon.

Christine still felt Erik's presence close by, heard Raoul frantically calling her name.

"I did not want to send your poem back," Christine spoke urgently into the smoke. "I had no choice."

When the air finally cleared, the gentlemen were crowded by the Opera Ghost's declared escape route, staring angrily across the room at another opened window. A gust of wind caused the heavy curtains to billow out tauntingly. Raoul raced to jerk aside the curtain and look out to the landscape beyond. Christine heard Raoul's frustration in the slam of his palm against the window frame. She did not have to be standing next to him to know that no one was in sight.

The Opera Ghost had vanished. Christine had no idea if he had heard her.

Chapter 12

"CHRISTINE? Are you awake?" Raoul stood in the doorway of Christine's bedchamber. The light from the hallway created a dark silhouette of his frame.

Christine lay unmoving, trying to decide whether or not to answer Raoul. She wanted to lose herself to the oblivion of slumber, but feared the nightmares that stole upon her defenseless mind. Asleep or awake, both realms held only misery.

"Christine?"

"I am awake, Raoul."

His sigh of relief carried across the room. "May I have a moment?"

"Yes." Christine sat up and lit a candle that rested on her nightstand.

With her long chestnut hair unbound and voluminous white night rail, she looked like an earthbound angel perched in her enormous bed. As he came closer, the candlelight cast an ethereal glow around Christine and revealed her eyes that pleaded with him not to hurt her again.

Raoul was jolted. *He* had put that look in her eyes? *He* had caused his precious Little Lotte pain? The last person in the world he would ever want to hurt looked at him as if she waited for his next blow. He flew across the room and knelt by the bed, clasping her hand to his heart.

"I am a beast. I am so very sorry, Little Lotte." He took her hand and rested his cheek against it. "I came in here to tell you how terrified I was when the Opera Ghost appeared. I thought I was going to lose you." Raoul stared up at Christine. "And then it struck me as I looked at you just now. I am losing you anyway, through my own actions. I don't know what came over me tonight."

Christine examined Raoul's countenance, looking for signs of insincerity, astonished by his admission. Minutes after Erik had made his reckless departure, Raoul bundled her up and whisked her home without a word to anyone, including herself. She thought his arrival in her room tonight meant that he'd finally decided to vent his spleen on her. However, the caustic Vicomte had vanished. Instead, *her* Raoul knelt before her in the secluded shadows of her bedchamber. She wanted badly to forgive him, but she had seen a side of him tonight that she hadn't known existed. He had forsaken her this evening. He had put himself and his wants before her, leaving Christine a victim to the sharp talons of his peers. And now he held her hand, penitent.

"Raoul, your behavior bordered on cruel tonight. I don't know who you are anymore." Christine said the words before she reconsidered. She did not want to smooth things over for him as she always did.

Bemused, he shook his head. "I am beginning to not recognize myself." He straightened and looked at the bed. "May I sit?" At Christine's nod, he settled on top of the bedcovers. "I don't understand what is happening, Christine. My love for you is unchanged. Yet everything is different. Why has it become so hard to be happy? Why is it that you and I are unable to maintain even a modicum of joy?"

A traitorous truth wrapped its sinuous length around Christine's mind. *Because we are hearts and dreams apart.*

No. She would not let whatever thoughts or feelings she held for Erik interfere with her marriage. Raoul was at last opening up to her, they were finally connecting again and still all that consumed her was her Phantom. She didn't know who deserved the title of beast more at this point.

Christine climbed out from underneath the covers and sat next to her husband. She laid her head on his shoulder. "I don't think either of us knew what to expect, Raoul. Everything happened so fast that we never thought it through. We never thought past the vision of you and I finally being together." She felt Raoul stiffen.

He turned her face to his. Shock infused his words. "Are you saying that this marriage was a mistake?"

That wasn't what Christine had been trying to say, but now she was terrified that if she opened her mouth to answer him, she would say yes. *Yes, this was a mistake, you are miserable, I am miserable. Our love is real, though it is the chaste love of friendship. I have tasted desire; I have felt like a woman in the arms of another man. True love is pounding outside on the walls of my heart demanding to be let in.*

A dam had burst inside Christine; she sat next to her husband, flooded and frozen with damning awareness.

"My God Christine, your hands are so cold." Raoul rubbed her hands with his own. He spoke quickly and with feeling. "We have been through so much together and I cannot accept that we have come this far only to cry failure. I love you, Little Lotte. I cherish you. I have acted in my own interests for some time. To be honest, I didn't want to believe that my own friends couldn't accept you."

Raoul jumped up from the bed, startling Christine. He paced back and forth in front of her and then halted. "I don't have all the answers at this moment. I-"

"Raoul." Christine motioned for him to sit back down. After he did so, she gave him a long look. *If I am to deny myself of everything that I am, then let my husband finally know me so I may find a measure of happiness within this marriage.*

"We exchanged vows, Raoul. I do not take that lightly. But our marriage is suffering." He looked as if he were about to cut her off, and she held up her hand to forestall him, her eyes imploring him to heed her words. "You always seek to shelter me from the harsher aspects of the world. It is an endearing quality, but a flawed reasoning. Because, I long for my husband to open up to me, to share his burdens, so that we may resolve them together. Raoul, you have been such a source of strength for me. I wished that perhaps every once in awhile I could provide strength for you as well."

Raoul tipped his head as if to prove he'd given all his attention to her words. When she spoke of providing strength for him, he smiled. "Little Lotte, you are such a gift. I would never think to ask that of you. It is my job to shield you from the harsher aspects of life." Too busy embracing her, Raoul did not see his wife's dejected expression as he effectively discounted everything she had asked him to consider. "However, I am very pleased to know that my wife takes her vows as seriously as I take mine. Besides a de Chagny would die before they would divorce."

Unease dripped down Christine's spine.

She pulled away from Raoul's arms. "That is not amusing, Raoul. I am trying to tell you that I want to share in this marriage equally and not just be a wife who needs looking after."

Raoul must have picked up on something in her tone. His smile became apologetic. "Forgive me. It was not my intention to make light of your offer or of your feelings." He stood and kissed her hand lightly. "I am going to take my leave now before I say anything else that might offend. You have had a rough night and need your sleep."

All hopes that her husband would at last look upon her as a helpmate and a woman vanished. His words were correct, but his tone rang with tolerant humor.

She moved back underneath the covers and lay down. "Good night, Raoul."

Before closing the door to her room, he murmured, "Good night, Little Lotte."

Christine watched the candlelight dance with the darkness and relived her surreal encounter with Erik. His macabre appearance and threatening behavior at the dinner party had not scared her. Instead, she ached with sorrow, for she could see how much he hurt, and his pain became hers as well.

The single flame from her candle burned steadily as did the emotion that she could ignore no longer. She welcomed it into her heart and for the smallest piece of time allowed herself the bliss of falling in love with Erik.

Christine leaned over to the candle and cupped her pale hand around the flame. She let the heat singe her just a bit. She pursed her lips, looking for all the world like a woman about to bestow a kiss, and then blew out the candle. Her world became black.

Chapter 13

RAOUL rose with the sun the next morning. He needed to take care of three pressing matters.

He increased the manpower and the perimeters in his hunt for the Opera Ghost. He issued an order for more doors to be knocked on, more questions asked. He planned to invest every penny he had if it would result in the death of this monster and a victory for himself. As he spoke with his man of affairs, his recounting of the Opera Ghost's actions maddened him to a degree that at times he could not think clearly, so powerful was the hatred and anger he felt.

Secondly, he sent a letter by special courier to Meg Giry asking her to call on Christine the next time she was in Paris. He would not issue Madame Giry the same invitation. Madame's patent unwillingness to help outraged his sense of honor and his need to guard Christine. Meg would put a smile on his wife's drawn features, and since more often than not she traveled with her ballet troupe, he had no concerns that she might encourage an association with the Opera Ghost. He also knew that Madame would never drag the daughter she had always sheltered into the nightmare of the Phantom. Yes, Meg was a safe way to bring Christine pleasure.

His last act involved sitting at his desk and creating a list of his esteemed colleagues and friends. As he read over his list, he asked himself if each person would ever accept Christine, and forced himself to honesty. He drew lines through every name that elicited a negative answer. When he finished, he was left with such a dismal number of people that might give Christine a chance that he felt a pitiful scarcity of friends.

Four days from now would be a true test. He had accepted an invitation to the opera from the Marquis de Ripon and his wife.

Raoul did not inform Christine of any of these things. He had promised to guide her and protect always, and he meant to uphold that promise with or without Christine's approval.

However, Raoul did intend to show his wife the importance he placed on her feelings by taking her on a shopping excursion. He prepared himself to let her make some choices, starting with her clothing. It would not be easy; Raoul came from a long line of de Chagny men who held the reins of their marriages with a firm grasp. But if allowing her to choose a gown or two would aid his cause, then he could loosen his hold a bit.

This would be the beginning of his efforts to demonstrate to Christine that he heard her and that he cared. Raoul felt confident that soon he would put an end to all the insanity that had invaded his life.

⸻

"Oh, *Mignonne*, it is good to see you." Madame Giry embraced Meg tightly.

Meg laughed. "Such a display of affection, *Maman*. I have missed you as well. Your letter was alarming in its brevity." She looked at her mother with concern.

Madame Giry smiled and smoothed away a strand of Meg's fair hair from her forehead. "I will explain in detail soon, *Mignonne*. Now tell me who you have fallen in love with." She laughed gently at Meg's surprise. "When you are loved, and love in return the whole world can see it. I am so pleased. Now come inside where it is warm."

They carried Meg's luggage to a cozy bedroom in the back of Madame's apartments. Her mother's black skirts rustled stiffly, a comforting, familiar sound to Meg.

As Madame unpacked, she told Meg all that had happened in

the past two years as far as Christine and Erik were concerned. Meg reacted with open-mouthed shock as she sagged down atop her bed. She still had only a vague notion of what had transpired before the opera fire. Her mother never wanted to involve Meg with that element of her world. As a child who already had to share so much of her mother with the other ballerinas, she had known there was yet another thief of *Maman's* attention and resented it. As an adult, Meg could see the love and wisdom behind her mother's choice and was deeply thankful, for this was a dark tale and Meg's life contained nothing but light.

A Prima Ballerina who traveled the world, she had the love of her leading man and before Meg left to visit her mother, she had received a touching proposal of marriage. She had so much, and she owed everything to this stern, caring woman who was her mother. For now, the news of her engagement could wait.

"What can I do to help?"

Madame gazed at her daughter and her heart swelled with pride. Meg's sweet face held only open concern. No shadows dwelled inside, no secrets shuttered her clear brown eyes. *At least I have succeeded with Meg*, Madame thought with a sharp pang, as Christine's look of distress flared to life in her mind. *And now I need one to help the other.* Madame sent a small prayer up to God for both Meg and Christine.

"Christine suffers greatly. She needs a strong friend right now. I am afraid that the Vicomte has ensured she has no contact with me. I would like it if you could to go to her and see exactly what sort of state she is in. I am sorry to ask this of you, *Mignonne.*"

Meg protested, "You have nothing to be sorry for. I will do whatever Christine needs. It means everything to me that you have this faith in me, *Maman*. I will not let either of you down."

A strange lump lodged in Madame's throat. She blinked away the moisture that rose to her eyes. "But I have always had faith in you. It is a mother's deepest wish to put rainbows on the horizon and keep the storm clouds at bay." A tear escaped as Madame smiled, wistful and proud. "I believe that you are more than ready to handle the rain, *Mignonne.*" Never one for flowery speech,

Madame promptly turned to face a large mirror that hung above a carved wooden bureau. With brisk movements she made a great show of tidying the tightly braided chignon she always wore.

Madame saw her daughter's fond grin in the reflection of the mirror and her eyebrows winged upward, daring Meg to comment on her mother's sentiment.

Meg picked up a blouse and folded it with careful creases, but her smile held. "It would appear that you and the Vicomte actually share the notion that I should be by Christine's side."

"Explain this, *s'il vous plait*."

"I shall do better than that." Meg fished a letter out of her beaded reticule. "I received this right before I left this afternoon." She handed the envelope to Madame and waited for her mother to read it.

Madame quickly read the contents. "*Mon Dieu!* This makes no sense to me. Why would the Vicomte invite you to see Christine?" Madame tapped her nail on the bureau as she deliberated. Her face took on a look of regret as understanding dawned. "I have always felt a measure of pity for the Vicomte. He seems destined to lose Christine, even when he has apparently won. Today my heart breaks for this man."

"*Maman?*" Meg fixed her concerned gaze on Madame's downcast expression.

Madame shook her head to dispel the cheerless notions that clung. "The Vicomte does not look past himself to see Christine. I think he is unable to put the faith in his wife that is needed to make their marriage succeed. I have the impression that he assumes I treat you in the same manner. That I do not take you into my confidence or consider asking for your assistance in any matter, especially the matter of Christine and Monsieur Phantom."

"Yet you have turned to me for help, *Maman*."

"I know that, *Mignonne*. It is a shame he does not. Perhaps if the Vicomte understood we cannot exist as entities unto ourselves all of the time, his marriage would not be in such dismal state."

"Come out of there Little Lotte, I shan't be kept waiting much longer! Don't be shy," Raoul cajoled.

Christine heard the amusement in Raoul's voice and then the answering giggle of the seamstresses. No doubt they fawned over her dashing husbands' every conspiratorial wink or flirtatious grin, while she hung back in the dressing room. But shyness did not keep her from moving forward, apprehension did.

Full of good spirits, Raoul had informed Christine that they would leave after breakfast to go shopping. Whatever fripperies she desired would be hers, all of her own choosing. It may not have been what Christine sought from her husband, but even to have a say in her own clothing meant a great deal at this point.

It would also keep her mind occupied while her heart accepted its fate. She was not up to the task of fighting both.

Thus far, things had gone smoothly. Christine had purchased gloves, hats, and shoes, even undergarments without a word of censure from Raoul. But now she stood inside the modiste's dressing room attired in the most sensual, exquisite gown she had ever worn off the stage.

In this dress of deep crimson Christine experienced the same heady emotions that she felt in Erik's arms. The image in the mirror showed a desirable woman, not a girl playing dress-up in her mother's clothing. She opened her eyes to the red-blooded female who felt lust, felt despair, felt pleasure and should be revered for all of those qualities. Should be, but was not. Not by her own husband, at any rate.

Christine could not comprehend why Raoul seemed so inclined to preserve the ideal of his childhood sweetheart instead of cultivating the interesting facets of his adult wife. She had grown to her seventh year listening to her father talk about her mother with such loving warmth that Christine had assumed all marriages contained the same fundamental affection. She wondered if Raoul was aware that the last time he had displayed any sort of true ardor was during the dramatic occurrences at the Opera House.

Each time he joined her in bed, Raoul ensured that the act contained no untamed desire, no urges that sapped one's control.

He treated her as a virtuous maiden in and out of the bedchamber much to Christine's surprise during the early stages of the marriage, and then to her increasing dismay later on. An appalled giggle of her own burst forth as it occurred to her that perhaps only Erik was capable of arousing both her and Raoul's passions.

"Christine? Oh, come now…it can't be that awful. Would you like some assistance?"

Christine stared at her reflection in the mirror to bolster her courage. The woman who stared back would not hide. She straightened her shoulders and glided into Raoul's view.

"Absolutely not," Raoul declared in a flat voice.

"And why is that, Raoul?" Pricks of temper sparked in Christine's voice. I am exposing far less than what most of your friends' wives do." She placed herself directly in front of the chair in which he reclined. "Look at me, Raoul. What about this dress is so unacceptable?"

Raoul's eyes traveled the length of his wife. The color of the gown enhanced her every attribute. Her hair took on a more lustrous quality, her eyes deepened in color and held self-assurance, the curves of her body promised rapture and Raoul could not accept that this fascinating woman was his Little Lotte. He couldn't bear the thought of her being anything more.

And suddenly he couldn't bear the thought of himself with that insight. "Choose whatever you like. Play the part of the strumpet or the parlor maid for all I care. I'll be waiting in the carriage." Raoul left Christine standing there with the dressmakers goggling at the Vicomtesse whose husband had just slighted her. Christine ignored the women, far past the point of caring what others thought of her. *If not the woman you married, if not the woman who wears this dress…then who are you in love with, Raoul?*

Whatever the answer may be, her husband needed to grasp the fact that his wife had another voice besides the one she sang with. Christine waited to hear the chiming of the little bells on the shop's door that would signal his departure from the shop. Instead, rapid footsteps heralded his return. Raoul entered the room, his eyes shadowed.

"You look breathtaking, Christine. Please see fit to order whatever else you find to your liking."

Christine's startled gaze followed her husband's exit. At first Raoul's erratic behavior these past few months merely confused her. Now, these increasing spurts of anger set her on the defensive, and it occurred to Christine that she no longer enjoyed the company of her own husband.

The bells on the door banged together, but did not chime.

Chapter 14

AS soon as Christine's smile of delighted welcome faded, Meg immediately noticed her lack of spirit. Beyond Christine's pallor and the downward tilt of her mouth, Christine simply seemed vacant.

They were ensconced in a lovely sitting room, waited on hand and foot by an army of servants, and Christine had never looked so wretched. *Maman* had been right to be concerned. Never before, not even through all the angst and fear that her friend had endured, had Meg seen Christine without some glimmer of life. In her heart she felt unprepared to face the changes in her friend, despite her earlier assurances to her mother.

"Meg, your visit here couldn't have been better timed." Christine's voice echoed with loneliness. "I am in need of a friend."

"Do you not have friendship with the Vicomte? I recall your saying how much fun the two of you had as children. Surely that is a wonderful foundation to build a marriage upon."

Slowly, Mignonne, do not push too fast. Meg could hear her mother's admonishment as clearly as if she were sitting right beside her.

Christine averted her gaze and plucked at the fringe on a pillow. "One would think so," she murmured.

Meg could not bear this insubstantial caricature of her dearest friend. "Christine? Tell me what is happening with you. *Maman* and I are so worried." Meg rushed on, "You have been my sister since that day you walked through the doors of the Opera House, and I cannot bear to think that you are unhappy. It is through both your husband and *Maman* that I am here today."

"Raoul asked you to come here?" Christine was shocked.

"Yes. I received a note from him yesterday. He is worried about you as well."

"As I am, him. I cannot credit that he would allow you to visit me when he has forbidden me any contact with your mother."

So, it is true, Meg thought, *Raoul's thirst for the Opera Ghost's head has turned him into a tyrant.* How unlike the adoring, affable Vicomte she had met two years before.

Or was he? Meg's mind flew to the past; even then the Vicomte had displayed a single-minded fervor in regard to winning Christine and ridding themselves of the Phantom.

"Are you still in love with him, Christine?"

Christine continued to toy with the fringe. A profound silence weighted the room down, broken only by the ticking of an ornamental clock. "Yes."

Meg had not expected that response; nevertheless she was pleased to hear that Christine still loved her husband. "Well then—"

"I am in love with Erik…you know him as my Angel of Music." Christine looked directly at Meg as she confessed her wonderful and terrible secret. To say those forbidden words aloud made her heart sing and her conscience shudder.

Meg covered her mouth with her hand, staring at Christine with dismayed compassion. Christine's eyes filled with tears.

"Do not give me any sympathy, Meg. I am barely able to keep myself from splintering apart." Meg paid no attention to Christine and laid a comforting arm around her desolate friend's shoulders.

"Raoul and I are mired in the shambles of our marriage and I don't think either one of us understands what went wrong…he won't even admit that there *is* something wrong. Now, I have fallen in love with not just another man, but the very one who my husband almost lost his life to, trying to save me. Do you still want *me* as your sister, Meg?" During her confession, Christine's body grew rigid; she wrenched herself away from Meg and sobbed, her entire body quaking with the force of her despair. Meg pulled Christine against her lending her warmth and strength.

"Shh, shhh…it will be all right. We will fix this." *Mon Dieu, Maman, how will we fix this?* Meg let her friend cry out everything that she had bottled up. She never knew that such misery existed, or that she would absorb it into herself through her love for Christine.

Finally Christine's tears slowed and stopped. Meg handed her a monogrammed handkerchief. Christine took it gratefully and dried her eyes.

"Meg, I am sorry to have burdened you with all of this."

"No, Christine. Sisters are always there for one another. You would do nothing less for me."

Christine's lips quirked at Meg's vehement tone. "There is no doubt of that. Thank you." She moved to hand the handkerchief back, and Meg saw her friend's gaze focus on the embroidered letters. "Whose initials are B.C.?"

Meg blushed. "That is my fiancé, Bernard Coutelier."

"Your fiancé? Oh Meg, I am thrilled for you!" Christine hugged Meg closely.

They drew apart. Meg worried her bottom lip. "I did not want to flaunt my glad tidings when you are suffering."

"Meg Giry, a sister always gains happiness from the other's good fortune. You would feel nothing less for me." Meg could see the sincere pleasure in Christine's eyes. "Well, tell me all about him."

Meg needed no further encouragement and happily poured out her story. "We have been in the same troupe for over a year now. He is a most gifted dancer. I think I truly fell in love with his talent first and then the man afterwards. We have so many of the same interests… when he proposed to me, all I could think is, I will be able to spend the rest of my life sharing the same dreams with the man I love. What better life could there be?" Meg's eyes were intent as she regarded her friend. "I would not give that up for anything, Christine."

Christine could not help experiencing a tiny sting of envy. *"I will be able to spend the rest of my life sharing the same dreams with the man I love."*

She marveled at the composed young woman who spoke of love and achieving happiness. It felt like only days ago when Meg knelt next to her in the cold chapel at the Opera House, looking at Christine as if she held all the answers.

"He sounds remarkable, Meg. Congratulations!"

Meg's eyes twinkled. "Would you like to hear something amusing?" Christine nodded, enjoying Meg's obvious delight. "When Bernard and I first met, he accused me of being a Diva! Imagine, me a Diva? I laughed for so long he became angry with me. Of course I told him all about our *beloved* Carlotta."

At the mention of Carlotta's name, Christine deflated.

"Do you know what happened to her after…after…?" She could not finish the question.

Carlotta had not only reigned supreme as the Prima Donna of the Opera House, she had also been romantically involved with her singing partner, the Opera Ghost's second and final victim of murder. Carlotta herself found her lover's body behind the heavy stage curtains, the Opera Ghost's signature Punjab lasso twisted fatally around his vulnerable neck.

"Christine, I wasn't thinking…"

"No, no, Meg. You simply took me by surprise. Please, do you have any news of her?" Christine held herself still while she waited for the inevitable account of Carlotta's sorrowful life after losing her beloved. Could this be a sign? This reminder of death that took place not so far back in time.

"Actually Carlotta is doing exceptionally well. Weeks after the tragedy, she received a large bank draft from an anonymous benefactor, which went a long way in healing her *broken* heart. I would not distress myself over that one, Christine. Women like her have only one concern in the world. How does this affect me? I hear she now has an American patron who is currently building an opera house in Boston, to be named after her." Meg sighed and took Christine's hands. "You would not love someone unworthy, Christine. From what little *Maman* has shared with me, I know he has suffered more than most. Why don't you tell me about Erik? Tell me why you have fallen in love with him."

Christine rose from the settee and walked to a window that faced a picturesque lake, complete with two gliding swans. The late afternoon sun dappled the calm waters. She touched her fingertip to the cool glass of the windowpane.

"He is the other half of my soul. I have never known such strength in a man. That he could take himself from the lowest depths of depravity and bring about his own catharsis and…this incredible man loves me; he desires me." Christine returned to Meg's side as she spoke.

Ah, there was that glow Meg remembered so well. "What are the circumstances between you two now?"

Raoul had been about to open the doors to join Christine and Meg in the sitting room. He stopped when he heard his wife's ardent words. "…

I am afraid I have wounded him past forgiveness. Since I was a child we have shared a connection, but I can no longer sense even that bond. He has withdrawn from me completely, save for his anger. I would go to him now if I thought there was any future for us, I would throw everything else aside, if I thought he could love me again. I realized too late how little meaning this life holds for me without him."

Disbelief coursed through Raoul. He closed his eyes against the crushing sorrow that invaded his soul.

In anguish he whispered, "My Little Lotte…"

He leaned heavily against the doors, unable to stand on his own, and replayed her words over and over in his mind until they took on one solid conclusion. After hearing Christine disclose her innermost feelings, everything held a pristine clarity for Raoul. He knew exactly what to do with his wandering Lotte.

His wife was adrift. She thought she had failed him; she loved him, and was now convinced that she had lost him with her recent conduct.

"I will show you the way back, Little Lotte. I will guide you for always."

Chapter 15

RAOUL had approached Christine in the greenhouse late in the morning to tell her he just received an invitation for a night at the opera, from his good friend, the Marquis de Ripon. He hastened to assure her that the Marquis' wife was a friendly woman who loved attending the opera, but for the most part, preferred country life to the non-stop whirlwind of city life.

"But the *opera*, Raoul…?"

He cast her a benevolent look, one of many that she had received in the past few days. "Little Lotte, I have given the matter a great deal of thought. Why should we deny ourselves something we take pleasure in? To do so would give the Opera Ghost power over us that he does not deserve. Besides, the Marquis' box is next to the Earl of Chester's. Perhaps he will attend as well and you can renew your acquaintance. He is quite popular these days."

Christine busied herself with the flower arrangement she had been working on and did not answer Raoul. Her chest tightened with apprehension. The Earl's box sat next to the Marquis's? Erik allowed no coincidences, and Christine would not fool herself into believing she knew what he would do or why he would do it.

As long as she continued in her marriage, as long as Erik held the title of Earl and Opera Ghost, as long as Raoul persisted in his hunt, as long as any of them still had breath in their bodies, this trap of deception and torment would ensnare them all. Christine found no consolation in knowing she could not have prevented any of this from happening; that fate could be pitiless.

But she could not base the life she chose on Erik's activities.

Erik could take care of himself, and Christine needed to follow that example.

Raoul reached to pluck a bloom from the arrangement and held it out to his wife with a boyish grin. She hesitated before taking it.

Raoul chuckled. "So serious. It is time we had some enjoyment. Let's do that, Christine, let's enjoy ourselves at the opera this evening."

Christine raised the flower to her nose and inhaled its engaging scent. Were they capable of enjoying themselves together any longer? Christine felt the memories of happier times pluck at her heartstrings. For that reason, she attempted to dredge up enough enthusiasm to both please her husband and bolster her false optimism.

"It sounds lovely, Raoul." Christine paired the words with a bright smile. But an awful sense of premonition told her that she and Raoul were not destined to enjoy themselves together. Ever again.

Raoul beamed in obvious approval. "Wonderful! You will have a pleasant time. I shan't let anyone or anything hurt you. You have to know how much I care for you; nothing shall ever change that." Raoul took the flower from Christine's hand and carelessly broke off the stalk. He tucked the blossom behind her ear and gazed at her with satisfaction. "Charming. Though it pales in comparison to you, Little Lotte. And these most likely will as well." Raoul withdrew a slender velvet box from the inside pocket of his coat. He opened the box to display a magnificent set of pearl earrings along with a matching pearl choker.

Christine reached out to touch the creamy pearls, her face alight with admiration. "These are exquisite, Raoul. What a delightful surprise."

"You should be aware that your husband is capable of many surprises. I thought you could wear them with that lavender gown we purchased in Vermeille."

Christine withdrew her hand. "Oh. I had thought to wear the dress I selected the other day."

Raoul frowned. "But the order hasn't even arrived yet. The modiste said it would take at least a week to complete."

So quickly they were back on the unstable emotional terrain that seemed to be the new hallmark of their marriage. Christine did not know where to step. *Just wear the lavender, Christine. After all, what is one more concession added to the heap that you have buried yourself under?* She thought of the crimson dress hanging in her wardrobe. Just knowing it was there made her feel stronger. She thought of Raoul's disapproval if she chose to wear it and disparaged herself for her failure as a Vicomtesse.

He would be better off without me as his wife, and yet he continues to try. Uncertain whether his efforts could be attributed to being in love or being deliberately blind, Christine experienced a sliver of apprehension as an unwelcome recollection made itself known. *"The de Chagnys would die before they would divorce."*

"Christine? How is it that you have the dress?" Raoul's tone now held a thread of annoyance.

"It is no secret, Raoul. There were only slight alterations to be made. It was delivered yesterday while you were out riding." Christine's tone matched his.

Raoul's lips tightened. He snapped the lid shut over the pearls and tossed the box beside Christine's flowers.

When he turned on his heel to leave, Christine grew exasperated. "Oh, for heavens sake, Raoul." He whirled around in surprise at Christine's outburst. "I will wear your precious lavender gown tonight. But if you will not allow me to dress myself, at least allow me the dignity of walking away from *you* right now." Christine snatched the pearls off of the table before she strode past her husband and out of the greenhouse.

Christine's fingers fumbled with the clasp of a luminous pearl earring as she tried to fasten it to her earlobe. After all this time, who would have thought she would be attending the opera again.

In short order, the earring was fastened. Christine did not bother with a last appraisal of her appearance before she joined her husband. She knew she looked the same as always, her style varied only by the shade of pastel. Raoul sought a watercolor, while she longed to be an oil painting.

He waited for her in the small parlor where she and Meg had visited days before. Christine noted with apathy how handsome Raoul looked in his black and white finery. But her temper flared when she discerned the gleam of victory in his eyes. She executed a mocking pirouette.

"I trust that I meet with your approval, Raoul?" Christine made sure her tone spoke in opposition to her words and smiled inwardly at his momentary expression of discomposure.

Raoul attempted to redirect her disposition with flattery. "You look captivating, if that is what you are asking. Thank you for wearing this gown."

Christine sighed. She was not a soldier, and she refused to let her marriage become a constant battlefield. She waved an invisible white flag and offered her capitulation. "You're welcome." She glanced around the parlor with puzzlement. "Why did you request to meet in here? Are we not joining the Marquis and his wife?"

"Yes, shortly. But we have enough time for a libation before we go. I haven't seen you since this afternoon in the greenhouse…" Raoul trailed off, waiting for Christine to express regret for her temper.

"I had to have this gown pressed and prepare myself for this evening. A sherry sounds perfect."

Though troubled by her lack of apology, Raoul's upbringing as a gentleman had him immediately responding to her request. He poured a measure of the dark liquid into a stemmed crystal glass and handed it to his wife.

He deliberated for a moment then picked up his own snifter of brandy and held it up. "A truce please, Christine. I was most sincere when I said we deserved some enjoyment tonight. While I acknowledge that perhaps I have some things to learn in regard to being a husband, could we please put this argument aside for now?"

Raoul's admission prodded at the dying embers of Christine's hope for their relationship. This was a first for him. Perhaps it could even be the initial small step toward the happier relationship they had once known.

Christine raised her sherry eagerly to toast her husband. "Yes, Raoul I should—" In horror she watched as her glass cracked against Raoul's snifter. The fragile stem snapped and the liquid contents spilled onto Christine's dress.

Her eyes flew to Raoul's face; he stared at the spreading stain with rage. Raoul struck what remained of the crystal glass out of Christine's shaking hand. Then he grabbed his handkerchief and mopped furiously at the sherry on her skirts.

"You did this on purpose!"

Christine backed away from her husband, trying to use her own hands to wipe at the stains. "No, Raoul! I swear!"

He straightened with a jerk, his expression one of livid accusation.

"Go upstairs and change, Christine. You shall have your wish."

"I-I don't understand."

"Don't you? You win. Wear your crimson dress to the opera."

Christine held her hand out to her husband. "This was an accident, Raoul. Surely you do not think I am capable of such low behavior?"

He coldly disregarded her words and her hand. "I honestly do not know what behavior you are capable of, Madame. We have people who are waiting on us, now go, lest you try my patience further!"

Christine fled the room without another word.

Raoul did not hear the door close as he stared at the disarray around him. His shocked gaze fell upon the broken stem that he had knocked from his wife's grasp.

The first time he took his anger out on his wife, he blamed it on the many pressures he'd been under. Now a second black mark marred his soul, and Raoul's stomach churned with disgust and a touch of panic. "I honestly do not know what behavior I am capable of either."

Chapter 16

GLOVES, cape, walking stick; the gentleman donned the last touches to his evening attire with a dry smile. After all this time, who would have thought he would be attending the opera again?

―

Raoul and Christine arrived at the *Opera Comique* just as the opening act of *Lakme* began. Raoul murmured their apologies to the Marquis and his wife as they took their seats in the darkened box.

The women sat next to each other in the front of the alcove, while their husbands sat in the chairs directly behind them. This afforded Christine a decent view of the empty box number five, some respite from Raoul's repressive silence, and a chance to truly relax and absorb the splendor of the soprano's voice.

Christine lost herself to the beautifully presented opera. Set in India, the story told of a beautiful young girl, *Lakme*, who fell in love with an English soldier and despite her father's murderous disapproval, they continued the courtship behind his back. Christine recalled Madame Giry saying once that it wasn't opera unless somebody died.

Even though she knew the tale would end in sorrow, Christine found herself rooting for the couple to triumph over the unkind forces that opposed their love. In the past she had enjoyed this opera for its numerous depths and its expressive songs. In her present state, she found she possessed a resentment bordering on anger for yet another saga of unrequited love. Still, the music held her in its powerful grip.

Intermission came too soon. Raoul and the Marquis escorted their wives downstairs for some champagne and made belated introductions. To Christine's stunned delight, the Marquis and his wife, Marie, a curvaceous beauty with laughing green eyes and a sleek cap of mahogany tresses, had been eager to meet her.

"We stay in the country for most of the year but happened to be in Paris the first night you sang. My dear, you were *magnifique*! Philippe almost divorced me to make himself available to you." Marie winked at her doting husband and continued, "Raoul is a smart man to have captured such a gem." She playfully tapped Raoul's shoulder with her fan to accentuate her point.

His lack of a reply went unnoticed as an attendant approached them bearing a tray of fluted champagne glasses filled not quite to the brim with the golden, bubbly fluid.

Marie sighed happily as her husband handed her a glass. "I adore champagne and I adore all things opera…the two combined? La! I am in heaven!"

As Philippe smiled indulgently at his wife, Christine saw precisely what he enjoyed most. She found herself smiling along with them, until Raoul held out a glass to her.

"Careful not to spill it." His face was a study in graciousness.

Eyes downcast, Christine took the glass with a quiet, "Thank you."

"Yes, do be careful. You wouldn't want to ruin that gorgeous dress." Unaware of the friction already between Raoul and Christine, Marie turned to her husband and batted her long eyelashes dramatically. "I shall perish if I do not get the name of her dressmaker. Christine is stunning in that gown! I am but a dowdy mouse in comparison."

The lovely Marquise took a forlorn sip of champagne. Her husband shook his head.

"Raoul, you must keep an eye out for the Earl. If he decides to make an appearance tonight, I shall have to beg money from him to support my wife's shopping tendencies."

Marie's expression turned from coy to indignant. "Shopping tendencies?"

The gaslights flickered signaling that intermission was at an end. The tall, debonair Marquis took his wife's arm and they strolled toward the staircase. He whispered something in her ear that caused her to laugh loudly and give him a flirtatious whack with her fan.

"They are wonderful," Christine said wistfully.

Raoul offered his arm to his wife. "Indeed."

Christine thought she detected longing in his voice as well.

The group settled themselves in their seats as the lighting dimmed. Onstage the velvet curtains parted, and the magic started all over for Christine. Thankful that Marie and Philippe were enraptured with the opera as well and did not use this time to fill the box with chatter as so many other patrons did, Christine turned to the stage.

Subtle movement in the balcony next to theirs caught Christine's eye. She turned her head at a snail's pace, not wanting to see what she had been secretly dreading all evening. A man sat in the Earl of Chester's box, his face turned attentively toward the stage. Without warning, Christine felt Erik's presence so forcefully she had no doubt—the Phantom had come to the opera.

She looked around cautiously to see if anyone else had noticed the occupancy of the Earl's box and caught her breath in dismay. Dozens of opera patrons trained their glasses on the Earl, trying to discern his features in the murky darkness. People whispered while pointing to where he sat. The general buzz that usually sounded from the audience grew louder.

"What the devil is going on?" Raoul left his seat and went into the hallway. Christine heard him speak with one of the attendants. She went rigid with fear. This was it. This night Erik would be captured and hung.

Raoul appeared moments later, a curious grin on his face. "I have news."

Philippe and Marie looked at him expectantly. Christine shifted her position to create an appearance of interest.

Raoul looked like a cat that had not only eaten a canary, but washed it down with a bowl of cream as well. "The Earl of Chester is here! It is possible that he will grant audiences to a certain few." He looked at Christine with challenge. "Perhaps you could use your connection with him to gain admittance to his box."

Marie clapped her hands together in excitement and stared at Christine. "You know the Earl? My dear, his name is on everyone's lips; even in our rusticated condition we have heard of him!"

Her husband cleared his throat. "I admit to being curious. He has gained considerable influence throughout Paris in a remarkably short time. I do believe you are the only person who has ever seen him! That is quite a coup."

"I cannot!" The two words rushed out of Christine with immense feeling.

Marie was clearly taken aback, as was her husband. Raoul looked disgusted.

Christine tried to clarify her rudeness. "He is very angry with me. I turned down his request to assist him in a school named after my father...Raoul and I have been trying to start a family..." Christine closed her mouth so hard her teeth clicked. Both she and Raoul turned the deepest shade of red.

Marie took pity on Christine. "Darling, that is completely understandable. I feel terrible that we pressed our wishes upon you! *Mon Dieu*, we have become gauche living away from Paris for so long." She patted the nearly nonexistent swell of her stomach. "Although, all that fresh air does wonders if a family is what you desire."

Philippe cleared his throat again, this time with censure. Marie tossed him an annoyed look. "La! Christine and I are already bosom friends. Come then, I should still like to try and meet the Earl of Mystery. Shall we try our luck, gentlemen?"

Marie all but sauntered out of the private box; the Marquis bowed to Christine and followed after his wife. Raoul left without a looking back.

Judging from the clamor down the hallway, it appeared that many people sought the Earl's notice. Christine shook her head in disbelief. *What are you thinking of, Erik? Run, escape…Go!* She lifted her own opera glasses and attempted a closer look inside the private box next to her. Her view no better than before, she only saw that he remained alone and blithely watched the performance!

"To love someone so much that you would choose death over existence without them. Such a tragedy…such a farce." The Phantom settled himself next to Christine and gestured at the stage.

"Erik?" Christine looked wildly at the man sitting beside her then back to the Earl's box where the gentleman still sat. "But who is that man sitting over there?"

Erik gave the barest of shrugs. "A fellow opera lover."

She knew he would say no more. "It does not matter then. You must go! They will be back at any moment!"

"Quiet, Christine. I am interested in hearing this duet."

"But you cannot—"

Erik unexpectedly switched his focus to Christine; he leaned close and placed a finger over her lips. "Shh" His eyes dropped down to take in her crimson gown, the rapid rise and fall of her chest over the scooped neckline, and then came back to her mouth where his finger still rested.

With sensuous worship, he traced the outline of Christine's full lips, and trailed his knuckle down the column of her neck.

The threat of Erik's capture, Raoul's imminent return, the great risk of discovery, all faded next to the heated pleasure that flowed through Christine. In this darkened balcony only she and Erik existed, it would always be thus, no matter where they were. A sense of intimate seclusion enveloped Christine, and she tilted her head back, allowing Erik better access to her flushed skin.

Something predatory and ravenous began to prowl impatiently within his soul. He did not pause in his endeavors as he then skimmed his knuckle over the curved flesh of her breasts that rose over her gown, felt her heart's rapid tempo; a match to his own. *Come away with me Christine. I love you.*

Love. The word startled Erik back to the reality of their bitter circumstances. He withdrew his hand and turned his attention back to the stage. With no outward signs of discomposure, he inwardly raged at his desire and weakness when it came to this woman.

"I used to believe that my curse was this face. Now I know that the true curse is my love for you."

"No!" It was a plea. It was a command. Christine tried to turn his face to look at her; her fingertips brushed the edge of his white mask.

Erik pulled violently away. "Do not."

"I wasn't…"

Erik glared at her. "Why did you look so miserable?" he demanded. "The night of that ridiculous party, why did you look so lost and alone? Why did you then, and still tonight, have such misery in your eyes?"

Christine stared at Erik in amazement. "That is why you are here?" When he would not respond, Christine pressed him. "You did not hear me when I told you that I never meant to return your poem? You came because you were worried about me?" Tears slipped from her eyes. "You risked your own life to…" She could not continue as the magnitude of his love felled her.

"I could not see you unhappy, Christine. Had I known about the poem, I would have come sooner."

"I am not worth it," she whispered. "I do not have your spirit, nor your courage, and I cannot say the words you deserve to hear because I made vows to a good man whom I mistakenly thought myself in love with. I am the veriest of cowards."

Erik braced his hands upon his thighs and stared upward at the ceiling, "Please, do not insult your worth to me." He gave a mirthless laugh. "I appear to be the one person on this earth who is aware of it."

His hand reached over to cover hers. Christine closed her eyes, savoring the contact.

"If I were to ask you to come with me tonight, what would be your answer?"

Her passionate declaration to Meg rang inside her mind, "*I would throw everything else aside, if I thought he could love me again."* But now that the moment had come, she knew she could not do that to Raoul. He had become as much of a victim as she or Erik in this merciless triangle. Christine did not trust herself however, if Erik were to apply even the smallest of pushes in that direction.

"Do not ask, Erik," she begged. Christine heard voices outside the hallway. Her party was returning. "You have to leave! Now… please…I could not bear life if you were to die."

Erik looked at her fiercely. "I can scarcely bear it without you now. What would your answer be?"

Sounds of a scuffle ensued right outside the curtains of the Marquis's box.

"For God sake, Erik, go!" Christine jumped from her chair and pulled on his arm.

He stood and held her in front of him. "Meet me tonight, Christine. Midnight at the school. We shall start a new life."

Christine placed a hasty, fervent kiss on his lips. "Please, if you love me, then go."

Erik eyes burned into hers, demanding an answer. The curtains behind them twitched as the fracas continued.

"Erik!"

He glanced sharply at the curtains and then withdrew a crumpled, folded piece of parchment from his breast pocket. Erik held Christine's gloved hand open and pressed the paper onto her palm. He let his own hand rest atop hers. "This poem is yours, Christine. My words will always be yours; my heart will recognize no other."

Raoul, Philippe and Marie entered the box in time to see the Phantom swirl his cape in a wide arc and leap over the balcony. The audience in the pit screamed in terror as a large, black caped figure slid down the length of a silk banner and landed gracefully on his feet. Only the performers onstage remained unaware of the drama unfolding outside of their own production.

With a wicked smile he threw a number of roses out to the

frightened crowd.

"Greetings from the Opera Ghost." Using the same flash and smoke technique, the Opera Ghost managed once again to elude any pursuers and simply vanished.

Christine sank back in her chair holding a single red rose. As she watched the last scene on stage, part of her mind saw only *Lakme's* pain; part felt only her own. *Lakme* had just learned her beloved was returning to his regiment. She was about to eat a poisonous flower that would result in her demise. Lakme chose death over life without her lover.

Furious, Raoul demanded, "Christine! What is the meaning of this? Why did you not call for me?"

Lakme ate the flower and died brokenhearted. End scene. Christine wondered what the flower tasted like.

She would not meet Erik tonight. The powers above were only inclined to grant them stolen moments. A life together—well Christine might as well wish to catch a falling star in her hands.

"Christine! I asked you a question!" Raoul's voice shook with so many emotions, it would have been impossible to siphon out even one.

Christine barely registered Marie's subtle motions to her husband that they should leave. Philippe's voice blustered down the hallway. "We are not allowed inside the Earl's box, then an elderly gent gives chase and engages us in fisticuffs. When we finally return to our own box, it has been invaded by the Opera Ghost…the poor Vicomtesse looks pale as death. What is going on?"

The gaslights flared to life and illuminated the theatre. Christine got to her feet resignedly. "I am exhausted, Raoul. Perhaps we could fight at home?" She brushed by him, still holding the rose.

―⁂―

Ducray opened the door for Erik. "Good evening, my lord."

Erik handed his cape and cane to the butler. "Good evening, Ducray."

"Did my Lord enjoy the opera?"

"I shall answer your question after midnight tonight."

"Very good, my lord."

Erik paused; Ducray bore the markings of a purplish bruise underneath his left eye. "Did my butler enjoy the opera?"

Ducray smiled broadly. "I did indeed, my lord."

Chapter 17

THUNDER roared and lightning split the black sky as the de Chagny carriage pulled into the yard. Christine jerked open the door and tumbled into the wet courtyard. Hiking up her heavy skirts, she raced inside the house without waiting for assistance. Raoul chased after her. Neither felt the biting sting of the rain as it pelted their faces or the winds that pushed.

"Christine!" Another loud crack of thunder punctuated Raoul's shout. He stood in the doorway, soaked from the brief run through the downpour.

A burst of lightning lit up the dark echoing space of the entrance hall. Christine glanced over her shoulder as she flew up the wide, curving staircase and saw Raoul eyes lock upon her moving form. Her sodden skirts hindered the attempt to increase her speed as Raoul stalked to the flight of stairs.

The butler hurried out, flustered and apologetic. "My lord, I did not expect you back so soon. Please let me take your—"

"There is no need. Go to your bed," Raoul snapped as he rushed past him.

Christine had reached the top of the landing when she felt Raoul grab her arm. She let out a scream.

"For the love of Christ, I am not going to hurt you, Christine!" The next clap of thunder caused the enormous crystal chandelier that hung from the tall ceiling to shudder ominously.

Wrenching her arm away from Raoul's grasp, Christine held onto the carved wooden post of the stairway's railing, while she fought to catch her breath. "Then why such fierce pursuit?"

Raoul took the last stair up so that he too stood on the landing. His own breathing labored in an effort to rein in his temper. "I am not a monster, Christine. I chased you because you ran from me, after refusing to speak to me in the carriage. You ran from me upon arriving…and all I would like to know is what in the name of hell were you doing with the Opera Ghost tonight?" Raoul's voice rose into a threatening bellow.

Christine had the disquieting impulse to step away from the top of the long flight of stairs. "You are frightening me, Raoul." She let only a hint of reproach shade her words so as not to incite him further.

Raoul eye's rounded in agony. He acted as if she had run him through as he crumpled to his knees onto the thick carpet. His head sagged from his neck, bowed so low that his hair almost touched her gown. Once upon a time, Christine would have run her fingers through that golden hair and comforted him. But now they stayed in their positions, dripping with rain and frozen with despair. She had no comfort to offer. Christine could not dredge up emotion from a well of emptiness.

Outside, the storm held its breath. Inside, an unnatural silence hovered in the air.

Raoul finally spoke, but did not look up. "You begged me once to save you from a world without light. You begged me to be your shelter…you needed my guidance and protection… that is what you asked of me and that is what I gave."

The truth of Raoul's speech tore at Christine's conscience. He had done all that she asked of him. "But we didn't know," Christine began without thinking.

"We didn't know what, Christine?" Raoul stood up with a wary look. His posture suggested a man who waited for the next thrust of a sword.

Taking a deep breath, Christine prepared to dust off memories she had stashed away in the catacombs of her mind. Memories that her husband would prefer to have long dead and forgotten. "You rescued me when I needed it most, Raoul, but we didn't know what this life would be like after we escaped. At the Opera House we barely endured in a world of madness and passion…we had to make choices with urgency…our every emotion heightened…all of us fought for a form of survival." Christine put emphasis on the word *all*.

Raoul ran his hand over his damp face as if he were trying to wipe her words away. "I used to understand you, Little Lotte."

"You did, Raoul—you understood Little Lotte. And that is perhaps a mistake on both of our parts. We knew each other best as children and then were strangers in love as adults. Have you not wondered yourself at times if we were better off unmarried? You cannot be happy with the way things have unfolded…your family, your friends and society at large shun me because I had the audacity to claim the title of Vicomtesse. And I cannot be happy knowing that it is because of me that your life has turned into this tiny, suffocating box with only myself inside as company for you. I was a dancer. I sang opera. I have no lineage to my name. You are a Vicomte born and bred. I feel so much guilt, Raoul, and I know you have regrets as well. Can we not speak openly with each other now, in this moment?"

The rain picked up and hammered against the windowpanes. Raoul straightened. A swift arc of lightning brought his features into view and for one instant Christine saw the man she fell in desperate love with on the roof of the Opera House. Raoul's face held all the devotion, the concern and passion that he had ever felt for Christine. Then the light was gone and the hallway contained only the two sodden figures and darkness. Christine shivered.

"You are chilled. You should change out of those wet clothes."

Relief swamped Christine at Raoul's concern. Surely this meant he was listening to her and needed some time. She would give him that time. "Yes, I would like to change into something dry. Perhaps we could continue this conversation tomorrow?" *Though, if I meet Erik at midnight, I will have no tomorrows for Raoul.*

"Perhaps, I have much to think on Lit—Christine. You have said so many things that I, too, felt but did not want to voice. I did not want them to become real, you see, and if I spoke these feelings out loud…" He trailed off as Christine gazed at him with sad understanding. Raoul cleared his throat and straightened his shoulders. "I won't detain you further."

On impulse, Christine hugged Raoul and his arms immediately wrapped around her. She felt a touch of moisture by her temple where Raoul's cheek rested and convinced herself that it was from the rain.

Raoul set her away from him. "I am going to find out why these blasted hallways are unlit. Good night."

"Good night, Raoul." Christine gave his hand a warm squeeze and started to remove her hand from his grasp, but to her astonishment, Raoul held fast.

"There is one thing I don't understand."

Thunder boomed and the storm released its breath in an angry howl.

"I heard you speaking with Meg the other day." His hold was firm, his tone bewildered. "You told her that you were afraid that I had withdrawn from you. And that you would throw everything else aside, if you thought I could love you again. Why did you tell her those things if you felt otherwise?"

With her stunned features hidden, Christine welcomed the darkness as her friend for the first time in her life. While Christine's mind and voice strove to respond with a believable answer, she thought she could actually hear the ideas and speculations in Raoul's head twisting and then fitting into place. Her own silence had damned her.

"And what of the Phantom?" Raoul inquired, his silky voice mere inches away. "You have not spoken of him, and yet he plays a most prominent role in all of this."

His total lack of emotion in such a dangerous question, and that Raoul still gripped her hand, caused Christine's heart to thump erratically in her breast.

"Raoul, I will answer all your questions after I change into some dry clothing."

"I think not. Please answer the question. Now."

This oily, constrained calm unnerved Christine far more than any of Erik's impassioned rants ever had. Raoul had no compunctions about intimidating her, and in recognizing that, Christine became tired of his bullying, tired playing the mouse to his tiger. *Let it be over now, these endless, painful fights.*

"No more questions, Raoul," Christine said with quiet conviction. "I am leaving. We cannot go on this way." Christine tried to pull her hand from Raoul's hold. Raoul only increased the pressure, forcing her to remain where she was.

"Raoul, you are hurting me!"

Several jagged streaks of lighting created a surreal effect. Dark then light—dark then light—Christine gasped as she looked at Raoul. Half of his face hid in shadow; the other half revealed features contorted in a vicious snarl.

The lightning ceased. As Christine and Raoul sank back into the blackness, an ominous swell of thunder began.

"You will not leave a de Chagny!" Fury finally loosened Raoul's grip.

Christine wrenched away to put some distance between them, feeling the haven of her room close behind her, yet unattainable. "Raoul, look at yourself…do you really want our marriage to turn uglier that it has already become? Please, I will go to Madame Giry's…we can talk when you have calmed down."

"If you leave me, I will not rest until your Phantom is dead."

Christine became utterly still. Raoul began to advance on her. "If you stay, I will drop the hunt. We shall live separate lives, but your life with have nothing to do with music, Madame Giry, or Meg."

"That is no life," Christine whispered.

Raoul continued ruthlessly. "If you violate that rule…I will make sure that the Opera Ghost is hung in a public square and left there for the world to see."

Either way I choose I cannot win. Christine wished she could rip her tortured heart from her chest; it served no purpose but to cause her pain and keep her alive in this decaying existence. *At least Erik will be free of Raoul…and free of me.* She would choose Raoul yet again, only this time she chose him for love of Erik.

"Very well, Raoul. You have made yourself a devil's pact."

"I did so two years ago." Without warning Raoul grabbed

Christine's arm and shoved her into her chambers. "No one is sorrier than I that this ugliness, as you call it, transpired. Yet, you show no remorse for your heart's infidelity, so I see no reason that "Honor thy wife" play a part in my life any longer." He withdrew a key from his pocket. "Do not expect an apology for my behavior. Good night, my *dear* wife."

The door shut, sealing Christine away from her dreams. The key turned, locking Raoul out of her heart.

As Raoul walked to his bedroom, he felt moisture on his cheeks and told himself it was from the rain.

At four o'clock in the morning, the Earl of Chester's front door crashed open. Ducray, who had been dozing in a rigid-backed chair in the entryway, awoke with a start. Thunder barreled and boomed. Lightning slashed and sizzled. The master had returned.

He stood in the doorway, a hulking, drenched figure. Behind him the storm had whipped up into its ultimate furious crescendo.

Ducray's eyes widened in apprehension, "My lord, did you walk all the way home?"

Erik's chest heaved in effort to release the breath he had been holding for what seemed like hours. She hadn't come. He entered his home with weighted footsteps.

Rushing to assist him, Ducray pulled Erik's soaked cape off his master's rigid form. "Am I to understand that the meeting did not go well?"

"The meeting did not take place at all, Ducray," Erik rasped. Those were the first words he had spoken since midnight, and they cost him. Erik was beaten and the Phantom was tired; both wanted to just lie down and be held in the arms of oblivion.

"Thank you for waiting up for me. I am sorry that your efforts tonight were for naught. Please, get some rest, Ducray."

Erik started up the stairs.

"Perhaps she could not meet you, sir. Give it a few days."

Erik paused on the steps. "I have already given her a lifetime."

Once inside his bedroom, Erik crossed to a large window that faced the direction of Christine's home. He watched the storm die while the tempest inside of him sustained.

"Three days, Christine. I will give you three days."

Chapter 18

CHRISTINE knew if she did not take advantage of Raoul's absence this day, she might as well accept her abysmal circumstances. Her panic for Erik's life had long since faded and she realized two things: that Raoul had used her biggest fear against her at her most vulnerable moment; and that she had been a fool to doubt in Erik's abilities to keep them both safe.

In these past few weeks Raoul had not ventured near Christine. His social activity resumed its pace as if he were a bachelor again. Christine noticed several new footmen around the premises, their eyes glued to her every movement. She had no issue with Raoul's avoidance, they had made an agreement, and in truth, she had not sought his volatile company for quite some time before her imprisonment. She did not quail at being a prisoner in Raoul's home; it was a prison of her own making, after all. But his visit to her rooms the night before brought about a desperate need for flight.

Raoul hovered by her bed, staring down at her. A lit candelabrum sat nearby. Christine had emitted a distressed shriek when her eyes fluttered open to this disquieting sight.

"Raoul? What are you doing in here?" She scrambled to sit up against her pillows. She doubted it was even two in the morning yet, an early night for him.

He sank down next to her and buried his face in his hands. "How has it come to this? We were so happy."

Christine could not agree with that statement, but she deeply mourned the end of her treasured, beloved friendship with Raoul.

He brought his gaze up to meet hers and dropped it back down again as if he did not like what he saw reflected in her eyes. "Were we not happy, Christine?" he asked unsteadily.

"Yes, Raoul...we were." *In the attic, while my father played the violin, we were very happy children.*

"And now it is too late...I have lost what I risked my life to save." Bitterness poisoned Raoul's declaration. His eyes held hers and pleaded for her to deny it.

Christine felt their mutual regret filling her room like a dense, stifling fog; she couldn't breathe anymore and longed for him to take his pleading looks elsewhere. Still, she couldn't help but ask the question that lay waiting in the back of her mind. "What did you love more, Raoul...me or the thought of saving me?"

"I loved you, Christine! Since that night I saw you onstage, since the days of our childhood, I have loved you."

"And yet you never sought to find me when Father died," she said in a low voice.

"I was a boy." Raoul's tone was incredulous. "You think to make all of this neat and tidy by claiming I never really loved you—because I didn't look for you when I was a child? Tell me then, Christine, how is it that you fell in love with me in such an instant on the rooftop? Were those feelings of yours a sham as well? Or perhaps we both experienced the same resonance of adoration that we had for each other as children, brought into the actualization of love when we saw each other as adults?"

Raoul's impassioned speech robbed Christine of her own voice. He had muddled her senses with his heartfelt honesty. To let these words in and see his point of view confused her further. Christine did not want to allow any shred of forgiveness for Raoul into her heart, not when she had steeled herself so completely against him since the thunderstorm. Pardon would bring about weakness, and weakness led to more hurt. But the thought would not leave until Christine acknowledged its humbling existence. Raoul loved her; he loved her the only way he knew how.

"Raoul...I am so sorry...I didn't know..."

Raoul pulled her against him and placed a gentle kiss on her brow, then, before she could stop him, rained increasingly ardent kisses over her face. "Christine."

Distressed at this sudden onslaught, Christine struggled to pull back, but Raoul held her tight. "Let me stay the night with you."

Her refusal pushed through the shock of such an intimate request. "No, Raoul. We are too far past that point."

He tilted up her chin and met her mouth with his. "Please Christine, one night, our last night…that's all I ask of you."

All I ask of you. The words haunted and condemned her this night. How could she refuse him? When had she ever refused him before? Weakened by forgiveness and burdened by remorse, Christine kissed Raoul once on his cheek. "Our last night, then."

Raoul gave a gentle nod in accord and lay her down against the pillows.

Christine's distress drained the act of all joy. They spoke not a word to each other. Nauseous, Christine felt as if she were betraying Erik in her husband's arms. She lay with Raoul like a vacant stranger.

For Raoul, their lovemaking was one last attempt at reigniting their relationship; for Christine, a dismal attempt at farewell to the one who had rescued her. Over faster than it had begun, cutting regret ridiculed their union.

Raoul got out of the bed and gathered his clothing, his movements agitated and hurried. Christine rolled to her side, unwilling to face him.

"You will not have to suffer through that again, I assure you." His voice sliced with winter cold. He slammed the door behind him.

The room fell blessedly silent. Christine thought of what had just transpired and waited for the sorrow to hit her. At the very least she expected to feel nothing; neither occurred. Instead, she began to tremble; the chill that Raoul left behind was soon replaced by warmth as a tiny fragment of something Christine almost didn't recognize grew and blossomed within her. Her heart thumped erratically and her nerves strummed with expectation. Then it came to her: this unfamiliar feeling inside of her was *hope*.

Christine let it saturate her; she wanted to drown in it. Hope, such a small word that held such enormous power. She was not ready to give up. She would go to Erik; Raoul would find a way to move on with his life… and each one of them would be happier for it. Hope, a promising word that enabled one to believe in fairy tales.

Though she possessed the desire to leave, Christine had neither a plan nor any means of escape. She glanced over to where a sizable traveling bag waited on her bed; she had packed it last night in a burst of anxious energy. She looked at her door and wished for a miracle to walk through and save her. A porcelain clock ticked off the minutes, the only sound in the room, aside from her breathing. Perhaps, if she could write a note to Meg, they would think of something. No, that would not work. How would she *get* the note to Meg?

With a knock and Christine's maid, Simone, spoke urgently through the door, "Vicomtesse, might I have a word with you?"

Christine grabbed the bag, threw open her armoire and stuffed it into the back. "Yes, of course, Simone," she called out.

The maid slipped into Christine's room. She peeked back into the hallway and then shut the door quickly behind her. "Your husband will be gone until late this afternoon." Simone gave Christine a meaningful look.

Christine had no idea why her maid shared this helpful news with her. "I see. Well, I appreciate your telling me this, Simone."

To her further surprise, Simone stepped closer and whispered, "I can have my Jean-Claude keep the new footmen distracted, my lady, if that is what you need. I'm not sure exactly what is going on between you and the Vicomte, but I have an idea. No woman should made to be a prisoner in her own home."

When Christine attempted to negate the comment, the anxious maid paid her no heed. "I owe you so much, my lady." Simone shyly extended her left hand to display a dull band of gold on her ring finger.

Still trying to follow the winding path of Simone's thoughts,

Christine was nevertheless delighted for her good fortune. "Oh, Simone! When did this happy occasion take place?"

Simone rubbed the ring with a wistful grin. "Three days ago, under the rose arbor. I see you are confused, my lady. Do you recall the day we were supposed to accompany you to meet that Earl? If you hadn't given Jean-Claude and me that time together...I do not think I would have ever gotten the chance to know him, save for the flirtation we often engaged in. So whatever you need to do now, do not fear from the servants. Do you see what I am trying to tell you?"

Freedom was at her fingertips!

"Thank you, Simone, thank you!" Christine gave the maid a fierce hug and ran to grab the traveling case out of her armoire. She halted on her way to the door. "Where are Raoul's footmen?"

Simone shrugged in a charming absent manner. "A fire has spread in one of the empty tenant cottages...everyone is needed to put it out. Bon voyage, my lady."

A small unconscious act of thoughtfulness had granted Christine her release from this luxurious prison. Fate tipped its hat to her as she rushed out of the bedroom and down the stairs.

A plain, black hansom cab waited for Christine in the drive. Simone and her husband had thought of everything. Christine fervently hoped that Raoul never discovered their duplicity.

As the cab drove away from the estate, Christine did not look back. She said a farewell to Raoul in her heart and prayed that in her absence he would seek happiness instead of vengeance. She did not need to look back at the place she had never considered her home. Christine would never look back again. The only thing that disturbed her was that she did not know what she had to look forward to.

Chapter 19

DISMAY filled Christine as she stared at Erik's school of music. From the window of the carriage she saw the padlocked doors. This did not bode well. Christine had expected a frigid reception, but no other message could have been clearer. Erik had effectively barred Christine from his life by shutting the doors to the school and to his heart.

She couldn't take her eyes off the building and swallowed with difficulty as grief knotted itself inside her throat. This would have been the starting point of her new life with Erik. How long had he waited? Did he go inside or stand on the steps in the pouring rain? The unwanted image of Erik waiting in front of the school soaked to the bone but uncaring, burned in her mind. Of course he stayed outside; a mere thunderstorm would not keep Erik from catching his first glimpse of her rushing to meet him—a dream realized.

Christine leaned back in the seat and closed her eyes. She had nowhere else to go but Madame Giry's, the first place Raoul would look if he searched for her. Christine did not want to endanger her friends; she had hoped Erik would be at the school. *And then what?* Christine laughed at herself. What had she hoped? That he would forgive her for the umpteenth time? That he would spirit her away and hold her in his strong arms until the end of eternity?

A ludicrous dream, but yes, that was what she had hoped.

The driver swung the carriage door open, startling Christine. "Mademoiselle, is this your destination?" His voice was impatient; she knew he had other fares to find.

"No…it isn't. However, I will need to disembark here. My

apologies." With no money left and no other option, Christine climbed out of the carriage and began the long walk to Madame Giry's address, dragging her heavy bag behind her. And as she trudged away from the school she thought of Erik; she wondered if the chains and padlock around his heart would prove as sturdy as those on the school's doors. She feared by now he would have destroyed the key.

"Christine! Come in." Meg ushered Christine from the evening chill into her mother's warm sitting room. Madame sat in front of a small, cheerful fire, mending a black skirt with precise, unhurried stitches. She looked up as Christine entered, and though her eyes registered Christine's bag, she showed no surprise.

"So, you have finally left the Vicomte then?"

Meg took Christine's bag and shot her friend a reassuring smile before leaving the room.

Christine removed her pelisse and sat down in a comfortable chair opposite Madame.

"Yes, I have left him. I am sorry for coming here because I fear Raoul will take his rage out on you and Meg. And I would never want to jeopardize the two of you."

"Rage, Christine? A strong word for your husband." Madame gave Christine a piercing glance. "He has not harmed you?"

Christine stared into the fire, replaying the various times Raoul's anger had gotten the better of him. Still, she suffered no physical blows. "No, Madame, it never came to that."

Madame sighed with relief. "Ah. I hope that you carry no other bruises save for the ones that dwell under your eyes. I would hate to think of the reaction someone might have if your husband had inflicted injury upon you." Christine stared into the fire and said nothing. Madame picked up an iron poker and prodded the logs. "And yet, there are different types of injuries, oui? This defeated posture of one of my best ballerinas would suggest so."

"When did he close the school?" Christine tried to keep the tremor out of her voice. Her father's school, Erik's triumph, ended, because of her.

Madame sighed again and pursed her lips, as if the memory created a bad taste in her mouth. "A little over two weeks ago. He sent a note to inform me. I have not seen him. Would you like to tell me what has transpired between you two?"

Christine sat upright and stared at Madame with surprise. She could not believe such a direct question came from the woman who had always worn her reserved manner like a badge of honor. "I would like to wait until Meg returns to impart the story, unless you think I should go?" Christine cast a worried glance at the doorway, half expecting Raoul to burst inside.

Madame Giry waved Christine's question away with impatience. "Do not be silly, Christine. You are as welcome here as my own daughter. I do not fear an angry Vicomte. But perhaps I could ask you another question while we wait?"

Madame raised an eyebrow at Christine's reluctant nod. "Why did you continue in your marriage even when you realized your heart belonged to Erik?"

"Meg told you of my feelings," Christine stated resignedly. She had known all would be relayed back to Madame Giry on the day of Meg's visit. However, in these past few weeks Christine had suffered from the awareness of her own folly. She did not wish to voice the reasons that once seemed so valid, for she saw them now as the reasons of a scared little girl.

Christine offered Madame Giry a partial explanation. "I take my vows of marriage seriously, Madame. Please do not fault me for that. Fidelity and love are not commonplace in the world I have inhabited for the past two years. What I felt for Raoul was far more than most of the woman in these circles will ever feel for their husbands."

Madame Giry set her mending aside with precise movements. "I enjoyed great love in my marriage, Christine." Madame waved her hand in the direction Meg had disappeared. "She will have great love in her marriage as well. It saddens me that you chose to remain perched in your gilded cage cleaving to empty vows, while true love flew past your window." Her eyes stayed on Christine, steady and questioning.

Christine wanted to cry out her innocence and explain that she hadn't had a choice. But her mind and her heart were in accord; Madame Giry had cut past Christine's shield of excuses and had driven home the truth with her unvarnished insight.

Meg's timely arrival saved Christine from having to respond.

"*Excusez-moi*, I was preparing your room, Christine. It has not been used in years. *Maman* cleans it regularly, but it needed a few touches."

"*Mignonne*, you are rambling. Christine will see her room shortly."

Christine watched as Madame's gentle admonishing look had Meg sitting down like a demure child. Something odd was afoot. "Whatever is the matter with this room?"

"In due time, Christine. Now, your story, please."

Christine's recognized Madame Giry's implacable tone all too well. She started with the episode at the dressmakers and finished with Simone's unexpected assistance. Christine could not bring herself to share the embarrassing details of the night before; only she need know that secret. Christine sat back in the chair feeling depleted, yet lighter. Meg's rapt face shone with interest; even Madame looked taken aback.

"He slid down the banner and tossed roses to the crowd?" Meg put her hand flat against her chest. "*Mon Dieu!* He has always been so dashing!"

"Meg!" Madame's voice was sharp. "There are other aspects to Christine's story that are far more compelling."

"I am sorry, *Maman*."

"It is all right, *Mignonne*. If Christine's circumstances were not so dire, my Frenchwoman's heart might also appreciate the Phantom's theatrics."

Christine interjected, "Dire, Madame? Surely it is not so bad?"

Madame slammed her hand down on her lap. "Not so bad? Christine, you have run away from your increasingly abusive husband, a man who currently hunts the man you love in hopes of catching and hanging him. I do not think Erik will particularly care if he is caught at this point." Christine tried to interrupt, but

Madame Giry would not have it.

"Despite the fact that you love him and know you belong to each other, you have broken his heart on three separate occasions. Three! And still he comes to you. Still he waits. You put yourself in front of him and make him hope. I should at least credit you with the fact that you haven't offered those precious words that he prizes more than his own life–three words he almost died from not hearing so long ago. Come, I will take you to your room. I cannot speak of this anymore." Madame Giry ended the conversation and stalked down the hallway, her limp barely noticeable in her agitation.

Meg reached to take Christine's limp hand. "Oh, Christine, I am so sorry. *Maman* did not mean those things."

Christine slipped her hand from Meg's grasp. "Yes, she did, Meg." She rose from the chair and moved to follow Madame. "Your mother has never wasted her words. It is just so hard to be certain what choices are correct. And these choices have such enormous consequences. What is so clear to those looking in from the outside is a tangled mess on the inside."

Meg listened to Christine's troubled speech and thought for a moment. "Then perhaps, Christine, you need to come outside and look for yourself." She led her friend down the hallway.

Christine stared in amazement as Meg showed her a hidden door in the linen closet. "This has been here all along?"

Meg nodded. "Oui. *Maman* will explain. Follow me."

They traveled down a small flight of wooden stairs and into a spacious room. Many candles burned throughout the chamber, making up for the lack of windows. They flickered merrily on the dresser, the nightstand, and clustered on a large oaken desk. A great four-poster bed stood to one side, the sheets turned down. Christine noticed with a pang that Meg had set out an ornate vase of colorful flowers; such a thoughtful touch. The pansies' sweet faces beamed with a happiness she had not known for a long time. The entire room invited Christine to lay aside her burdens and rest.

She stopped her perusal short as awareness lifted the tiny hairs on the nape of her neck. Christine knew why this room existed, who it had been created for.

"This is where he slept."

Madame came behind Christine and laid a hand on her shoulder. "*Oui*. This is where he slept and this is where he almost died." Christine's eyes glistened with tears. As if she sensed Christine's dismay, Madame patted her shoulder and crossed over to the bed. "I do not blame you for that, Christine. He did not allow you any other option. Had you stayed with him, it would have destroyed you both."

"But you blame me now?" Christine's wounded gaze locked on the woman who had provided guidance when Christine had no one else.

Madame shook her head. "It is not a matter of blame. It is a matter of taking the reins and having the courage to stay on course. You alone have to do this, Christine. You have discovered love in your heart for Erik, but now you must locate the strength to embrace the unknown with the man you love by your side."

"But he has closed the school; it is too late." The scared little girl crept back and wanted to hide underneath the covers. "Could you go to him and ask that he reopen it? I could meet with him there…"

"I will not. Nor will Meg." Madame shot her daughter a quelling look.

Meg shrugged. "I agree with *Maman*, Christine. You have to go to him. He has come to you so many times. If that wonderful school is to be reopened, then it has to be you who asks."

Christine scrambled for excuses. "What if he won't see me? What if he won't listen?"

Madame frowned, "As long as you can get past that impudent butler, Erik will not turn you away. He has never turned you away."

Christine accepted the significant reminder with sudden grace. This was no time for retreat; it was time to grow up. "Very well. I will go to Erik. If I have taken the drastic step to leave Raoul only to be deterred by a set of locked doors, then I deserve nothing less then the same heartache I have caused." Stirrings of panic ebbed and flowed in her belly at the thought of laying herself bare to Erik's scorn; she tamped them down with difficulty. "I will go tomorrow before I change my mind."

Meg clasped her hands together in relief. "You are doing the right thing, Christine. I will be here for you no matter what the outcome."

"As am I, *Mignonne*." Madame Giry cupped Christine's cheek gently. "It will not be easy. But things worthwhile seldom are."

Christine's heart swelled at the endearment that Madame normally reserved for Meg. She took a deep breath, then exhaled, wanting nothing more now than to be alone in the room with her thoughts of Erik. Perhaps being in this room where he had almost found death, but instead discovered strength, would give her the fortitude she needed to see him on the morrow. "I would like to lie down for awhile before dinner."

Meg and her mother nodded their understanding and turned away.

As they climbed the steps, Christine called out. "Madame, why did you refer to the butler as impudent?"

Meg's laughing answer put a smile on Christine's face. "It would seem that he has developed a tendre for *Maman*. They met at the school and now the man writes her the most romantic love letters."

Christine heard Madame Giry shush her daughter sternly and stomp up the staircase.

Chapter 20

DUCRAY answered the door. A credit to his position, his face revealed naught at the sight of a young, unescorted woman standing on the doorstep.

"Good afternoon. May I help you?"

Christine gave the austere butler a nervous smile. Surely this fellow could not be the author of Madame's love letters. "I am looking for the Earl of Chester. Is he in?"

"May I tell him who is calling?" Ducray made no move to let her enter.

Christine studied the barely discernable glint in his eye. She suspected that this servant knew exactly who she was. "Yes, please tell him that…Christine is here to see him."

Ducray looked down the length of his hooked nose at her. "Indeed. Please follow me."

They walked though the imposing front entrance and down a dimly lit corridor. Christine noted many unusual paintings and exotic objets d'art. She wondered if the items reflected Erik's travels or if they were adornments from the previous Earl.

Ducray came to a halt in front of a set of thick doors. "My apologies, Madame. May I have your name again?"

At the use of, Madame, a married woman's title, Christine had no question that he knew her name. Still, she answered for the second time. "My name is Christine."

Ducray threw open the doors to Erik's study and announced, "The Vicomtesse de Chagny here to see you, my Lord." He stepped to the side to allow Christine entrance.

She stepped tentatively into the room, her eyes searching for Erik.

She saw him at his desk, writing. As usual even his smallest act contained a hum of intensity.

He looked like a pirate scholar. The top buttons of his linen shirt left were left undone. Though Erik's head was bent in seeming concentration, Christine could see his face remained uncovered. Even the dark hairpiece that always seemed such a natural part of him, held a rakish look of dishevelment.

Erik at last looked up from his correspondence to rest his intense green gaze on Christine. She endured the weight of his stare for several minutes before he said, a defined sneer to his lips, "My dear Vicomtesse, braving the beast in his lair? To what do I owe this new torment?"

A muffled click signaled Ducray shutting the doors, leaving Christine and Erik alone together, yet fathoms apart.

Behind Erik, Christine saw a massive wall covered with masks. Some were hideous, some were plain, most were uncommonly beautiful. Christine marveled at the vast collection. She did not recognize the majority of the masks, but some she did, and each of those held an extraordinary, though sometimes disturbing memory for her.

Her nerves stretched and tightened, as did the silence. Finally, she tore her gaze from the display and forced herself to face Erik. He locked eyes with her, then rose from behind the desk and allowed Christine to behold him, completely unmasked and utterly heartbroken. She watched the tragedy of their lives unfold in his eyes, a series of memories, each one holding the promise of bliss but inevitably ending in tears. He willed her to see his torment and held nothing back. Christine bit her lip to keep from crying out her own heartache at the depth of his suffering.

He turned to the wall and chose a plain, white mask, most severe in its simplicity. Holding it inches from his countenance, he once again faced Christine; with deliberate movements Erik secured the mask over the damaged part of his face, making sure she understood his every movement. He walked around to the front of his desk and leaned against it, then crossed his arms, creating an intentional barrier.

The Phantom had returned, and forgiveness was not in his repertoire.

Christine had come prepared to absorb anger, hurt, and accusations and, with luck, work through them with Erik. But this Phantom, who watched her as a falcon does a rabbit, was altogether merciless.

She spun around to escape and heard his smooth whisper carry across the room.

"Coward."

Her spine straightened with the rigid precision of a dancer. To hear him, of all people, label her thus was intolerable. Her mind went to the night at the opera when he spoke of her worth; she had been staggered that he held her in such esteem. Perhaps she had come too late to regain Erik's respect, but Christine felt that she owed it to both of them to let this meeting run its blind course. Now she must reach inside herself and know her own value.

She pivoted on her heel, her tread wary as she approached his desk.

The falcon watched the rabbit cross the open field, nothing to protect it from its waiting talons.

Christine positioned herself in front of him, an arm's length away. She felt so terribly awkward and unsure, and the Phantom gave no quarter. Her heart mustered up expressions of contrition and love, but her mind took over and had her blurting out, "I have come here for one purpose. I have a favor to request of you."

The Phantom's eyes shuttered and Christine knew she had bungled her words, her very first words to him, badly.

"A favor, you say?" The Phantom pushed away from his desk and began to circle Christine. He pressed his fingertip to his temple as if in great deliberation. "Now let me see...I could teach you to sing and give wings to your soul—No! That is simply not good enough." Christine stared straight ahead, trembling. The Phantom stopped in front of her. "I have it! I shall create a school of music to honor your beloved father and yourself. No, no...that is not acceptable either."

He resumed circling. "This is certainly a difficult endeavor, Vicomtesse—but wait! Perhaps if I ventured into the hell of my own soul and forged a better man from that hell for want of your love, that would be considered a great favor?" The Phantom shook his head. "I am very close right now, I can feel it…"

Stalking over to his desk, he pulled open a tiny drawer from which he withdrew a sharp, jeweled dagger. "Ah." He brought the dagger to Christine and held it out like an offering. She flicked her nervous gaze from the shiny blade to his grim features. The Phantom took her hand and closed it around the handle of the dagger. He did not let his touch linger. "I now understand what it is you need. Giving you my heart wasn't good enough…you would like to carve it out of my chest!"

"Stop it!" Christine dropped the dagger and let it clatter to the floor. "Stop it…please."

"Get out of my home!" he roared.

Christine flinched but did not back down. "I came here to ask you to reopen the school. It is a travesty to close such a thing of beauty."

"And yet beauty and travesty survive together on a daily basis." The Phantom behind the mask mocked her. "The school will remain closed. I will have no part of that idiocy. You came here on a fool's quest, Christine. Now leave." He sat down at his desk and resumed his writing as if nothing untoward had rippled his morning activities, as if Christine were not even there.

If he had not spoken her name, Christine would have left. But he had and that lent her the nerve to sing.

"Look at me,
Look at me, Erik
Please, don't turn from me.
You've changed, you say,
My only hope
In my hour of need.
Please realize

Why I denied my soul
I could not bear to be untrue
Will I ever find forgiveness
Once again from you?"

As she sang she forgot her purpose. All that filled her mind was how Erik had always loved her voice, had always loved her. Her song became a gift and an apology, each chord perfection. Heaven had opened its gates and let the notes fall, like the sweetest drops of nectar, over and around Erik.

She used the most exquisite weapon in her arsenal—her voice.

A velvet pouch landed by Christine's feet, "That is the key to the school. Ducray will show you out." Erik would not look up.

Christine stared at the top of Erik's bent head, too much still left unsaid. She clutched the pouch to her chest. Everything she wanted to explain, the love she felt, pressed to be voiced. *If he looks up at me this moment, I will tell him. If he stops shutting me out with this fearsome coldness, I will be able to open up. Please Erik, one more glance, one more chance to look into your eyes right now.*

The scared little girl tugged on her skirts. Knowing she must retreat, Christine paused for the space of a heartbeat. Erik continued his correspondence. Their meeting was over.

The key felt large and solid within the velvet confines of the pouch. Christine's grasp was tight around it, and she was reassured by its weight as she walked out of the study.

Keys were meant to unlock things. Keys were meant to open doors.

Erik waited long minutes until he was positive she was gone and that he could trust himself not to go after her. Within the first lilting words of her siren song he knew he had lost. He drew idly with his quill as he waited for the maddening urge to pass. His soul finally quieted, and he removed the mask from his face, placing it on the desk.

Why did she have to come here? The last place that held any sanctuary for him? He never returned to his lair underneath the Opera House; he refused to set foot in the school. Anywhere that she had been, he could see her, feel her, and taste the very air around him with her essence. And now she had filled the dark corners of his home with her special light, for even at her dimmest, Christine contained a glow to which he would always be helplessly drawn.

Erik's mind raced. Perhaps he should have talked to her; perhaps he should follow her now and demand answers. He stood, and his eyes fell to the dagger that lay on the floor. His traitorous heart gave a painful lurch, and he willed it to stone again.

"Impudent lass!
This Little Lotte
Asking for my pardon!

Unfeeling girl!
This brazen Vicomtesse
Daring to come to me!"

He lay his shaking hand over the ravaged area of his face.

"I was her Angel of Music…"

Chapter 21

IRONICALLY, Raoul had no knowledge of Christine's absence until four days came and went. He had taken advantage of an open invitation to stay at a friend's residence whenever he visited the city of Paris.

He availed himself to the endless carousel of distractions and gatherings. If anyone inquired about his wife, an occasion which rarely happened, he informed them that she was quite ill and would be confined to her bed for an indefinite amount of time. His circle of friends did not appear to be displeased with the news and did not press him to speak of her further. Raoul spent the four days reveling in the festive atmosphere of the present while trying to bury the haunting disgrace of his recent past.

He arrived home in good spirits, feeling that he could face Christine again. Once inside, he noticed the silence, though not the everyday type of silence he had become accustomed to. With only two people besides the unobtrusive servants in such an enormous house, one became used to a degree of quiet. But this stillness unsettled him; his home felt like a puzzle missing its last piece.

"Christine," he breathed. Raoul ran up the stairs, taking them two at a time. The uncontrollable, gnawing fear that had lived inside him since he had seen the rose on the balcony mushroomed into choking dread when he reached her room and banged the door open. "Christine!"

Her complete absence greeted him. Raoul ripped open the door to the closet still packed with her gowns. He tugged opened drawers that still held her belongings. Not an item disturbed, but he knew Christine had managed to leave him.

Disbelief and rage clashed in his head. Raoul squeezed his eyes so tightly that small pinpoints of light danced behind his eyelids. When the clamor in his mind finally died down, he reopened his eyes and surveyed the room. Strange. If he hadn't touched the closet or the drawers, this feminine, frilled chamber would be immaculate. It would look untouched, as if Christine had never slept here and called this room her own. It would look as if it still waited for a Vicomtesse to claim it. Christine had not left her mark upon the chamber, merely indelible scores upon his soul.

Raoul did not know what to do. For the first time in his life, he did not have a plan or an action to take. Dazed, like the time he had fallen from his horse as a boy and hit his head on the base of a large oak; Raoul suffered the same feelings of nausea, dizziness and pain.

Simone came hurrying into the room and let out a screech when she spotted him.

Raoul stared thoughtfully at Christine's personal maid, who stared back wide-eyed and unmoving. He would start with some questions.

"Simone, is it?"

She jumped, "Y-yes, my Lord."

"Where is the Vicomtesse?"

To his great discomfort, the maid lurched toward him, clutched at his lapels and started bawling, huge gulping sobs that watered his shirtfront. "Come now, please try and pull yourself together. Where is my wife?" He set the maid away from his person and took a step back as if to remind her the marked difference of their social standing.

Simone babbled almost incoherently. "There was a fire... tenant's cottage...everyone needed...came back...my lady gone..." Her sobs renewed with even greater force. "I am s-sorry my lord, p-please do not dismiss me!"

Raoul wanted to get away from this clutching, crying woman. She was of no value to him. "You will not lose your position. I will have my wife home where she belongs by tonight. She hasn't been herself lately; it is important that we do not let her stray from the protection of the house. She could get hurt."

"Is she ill, my lord?" Simone wiped at her tears with the back of her wrist as she asked the question.

Raoul's eyes darted back and forth over Simone's head as an idea caught and spread through his mind. "I would not say she is ill, precisely. But I would not be surprised if there is another addition running through these halls in the near future. That is why we must take extra precautions with our mistress when I bring her home. As I said, she is not quite herself." He patted her twice on the shoulder, confident he had planted the correct seeds. With the servants' support he could ensure Christine would never escape again. He should have thought of this sooner.

"Please prepare the Vicomtesse's room as usual Simone, I suspect she is at her friend's home and is waiting for me to retrieve her." *Madame Giry will pay dearly.*

Simone sniffled loudly and Raoul handed her his handkerchief, his expression of distaste taking away from the thoughtfulness of the gesture. She blew her nose and gave him a watery smile. "You must love her very much to take such care of her."

He felt as if she had struck him across the face. *Love?* The word hadn't entered his mind once since he had realized that Christine left him. Even on the night of the storm when she had stated she wanted to leave, love had not entered his mind. Keeping what was his had been the driving force. When had Christine become a possession instead of a person?

I will think on this when I get her back. Raoul never answered Simone; he shook his head distractedly and stalked out of the room.

As soon as the Vicomte exited, Simone's tears dried. She had been the Vicomtesse's personal maid for two years. Her mistress could not possibly be with child and Simone be unaware of it. She raised her eyes heavenward and sent up a prayer for Christine. "May God grant you strength. May fate steer your path to joy."

"Ah, Vicomte. Is this to be a repeat performance?" Madame Giry opened the door to allow Raoul inside.

He did not move from the threshold. "I am looking for Christine this time Madame. If the Opera Ghost is here as well, then that would make my life so much easier."

"I am sorry to disappoint you on both counts, monsieur." Madame's eyes spoke volumes of a different message. "It is only myself here. Meg left early this morning to rejoin her troupe."

Raoul cast Madame a triumphant smile. "I thought you might say that." He stepped to the side and several policemen burst into her apartments. "Search the entire premises."

"You have no right!"

"On the contrary, Madame, I have not only the right, but I have every intention of exploiting that right to it's fullest." Raoul shoved a document under her nose and experienced a thrill of conquest when her hand gave a noticeable tremor as she took the paper.

When Madame finished reading it, she handed it back to him. The only emotion Raoul could discern was contempt. "So, now you use the law to do your work. I wonder, Vicomte, when did the dashing hero on the white horse turn into the spoiled Lordling who uses purses of gold to terrorize a woman living alone? Your money may have bought you the right to invade my home, but it will not bring back Christine, and it has never been of any use when trying to capture the Opera Ghost." Madame gave her back to Raoul. She chose a gilded, stiff-backed chair, settling herself like a queen.

Thwarted at every turn, Raoul clenched his jaw, knowing his face must be livid. First the Opera Ghost, then Christine, and now this ballet instructor ridiculing him, making a fool of him—the Vicomte de Chagny! Raoul cursed the day he ever set foot in that foul Opera House. His hands twitched and a red haze veiled his sight. In his mind, Raoul could picture himself wrapping his hands around Madame's throat and squeezing until she told him everything she knew or died because of it. The vision ended in the blink of an eye. He must have emitted a slight noise because Madame eyed him questioningly.

"A glass of water monsieur? Your police should soon be finished, but it is no trouble."

Raoul stared back at her, paralyzed with shock. He had just imagined himself strangling this woman. He reeled with the knowledge that he was capable of such monstrous thoughts.

"Vicomte?" A note of concern entered Madame's voice.

The sound of heavy footsteps in the hallway snapped Raoul out of his stupor. He looked around like a fox whose hounds were fast approaching.

A large fellow came into the parlor with the other officers close behind. "We found no one here, my lord, nor are there any signs of someone having recently been."

Raoul glared at Madame Giry. "This is not over. I will find Christine; it is only a matter of time." His voice was brusque.

Madame pulled herself to her feet and gave the Vicomte a curious look laced with pity. "And then what will you do with your runaway Vicomtesse, my Lord? What will you do with a woman who does not love you anymore?"

The policemen took their leave, each one hurrying outside as if he had remembered urgent business; each counting their blessings that their lives and wives were uncomplicated.

Raoul and Madame stared at each other. Raoul let out a deep breath. "I do not know," he answered sadly.

"Then perhaps it is best that you let her go," Madame Giry suggested, her words mild.

The red haze returned at the thought of giving Christine up, at the thought of losing. "Never!"

This time when Raoul slammed the door behind him, the figurine of the opera singer tumbled from the shelf and shattered into the tiniest fragments.

Chapter 22

IF not for a stone caught in her horse's shoe, Raoul might have discovered Christine's whereabouts.

On the morning after Raoul's hostile appearance, Christine borrowed Madame Giry's small gig and set out for the school. Halfway there she realized she had forgotten her apron and turned around. Christine had no desire to ruin one of the few dresses she'd brought with her. These past few days had given her a healthy respect for cleanliness.

Some of the smaller side chambers in the school that Christine had set aside for storage were buried under years of filth. After the emotional turmoil of her encounter with Erik left her confidence in tatters, three days of vigorous cleaning was precisely the kind of mindless activity she had needed. And when it occurred to her that these labors were a penance for the hurt she had inflicted on both Raoul and Erik, she scrubbed even harder.

Each evening she would return to Madame Giry's with barely enough energy to eat. After minimal conversation and a bath, Christine would seek her bed. And while she slept surrounded by Erik's lingering presence, her soul would fulfill her deepest desire through dreams. It was always the same simple dream, consisting of a shared life with Erik, waking up next to Erik each morning, and smiling. In her dreams they always smiled.

Her experience this morning led her to leave Madame's house earlier than usual. Christine had awakened with the joy still in her heart; she fully expected to see Erik's sleeping form next to her. Reality was her only bedmate, and it ripped through the last gossamer strands of her fantasy.

She was a married woman in love with another man who despised her. The closest she would ever be to waking up with Erik was sleeping in this bed he had once slumbered in as well. The closest she would ever be to sharing a life with him was by continuing the vision of the music school in his absence.

So, Christine had left early that morning, hoping to leave her demons behind. And now, because of her forgetfulness, she would need to return. She had reached the end of Madame's street when the horse faltered and let out a small whinny. Christine pulled the gig to a gentle stop and climbed down to inspect the hoof that the horse appeared to favor. A small stone had lodged in the poor beast's shoe; Christine carefully released the hoof and patted the horse's neck. She took the reins and led the horse in a measured walk back toward Madame's residence.

Then she stopped. A figure, obviously a woman by her dress, stood in front of Madame's walkway searching through her reticule. That wasn't what had Christine pausing however; she knew that it was Madame Giry's maid who came twice a week to clean the apartments and take care of any shopping. A stocky man marched from across the cobblestone street, and Christine almost called out in warning. Instinct clamped her mouth shut at the last second. The man's approach seemed officious, his walk determined, but not threatening.

Whatever he said to the maid had her shaking her head and speaking rapidly, her hands like wild birds fluttering around her. The maid's words appeared to satisfy him; he gave her an abbreviated bow and returned to a shiny, black carriage Christine had not noticed before.

Did Raoul hire someone to watch the address? Madame had warned her that he would not give up. And while Christine cursed him for his inability to release her, neither could she blame him for his actions. She had left him in the same unsettled state of being with which she'd burdened herself. Though floating aimlessly apart, they were chained to each other through matrimony, and Christine wondered what it would finally take to sever the binding, iron links. And while she took the time to sort this out, she would not take any chances upon Raoul discovering her whereabouts.

Christine clicked softly to the horse and led it down a small side street to a concealed side entrance, which Madame Giry had arranged for Erik's convenience. She now lived a Phantom's existence. An empty chuckle had the horse swinging its large head to gaze at her as they walked.

Following the incident with the maid, Christine and Madame Giry took extra precautions when venturing out. They always left at the same time. Madame rented another carriage and made it a point to leave from the front in an obvious manner. Every morning she shut the door with a bang, her heels tapping loudly on her stone walkway as she approached the hired cab and then called out to the driver with a hale, "Good day, Monsieur!"

Madame never acknowledged the man in the black carriage nor gave any signs of noticing him. Christine would slip out the side entrance and take the small gig through back streets and small avenues to reach the school. Women who traveled the streets of Paris alone left themselves vulnerable to danger, but both Christine and Madame Giry felt that the threat from Raoul was far greater.

Thus, they established a pattern, and a week had passed. Madame had finished reviewing the long list of applicants and now set her mind to writing the necessary responses. Christine had run out of rooms to clean at the school, and her mind had taken up the most annoying habit of making her believe that Erik would walk through the doors at any moment. She had been so certain he would appear, if only to rage at her.

What else was there to do? Unwittingly Christine's eyes fell to the stage, and she looked quickly away. But the notion persisted and Christine experienced a surge of adrenaline.

"Madame?"

Madame Giry glanced up from her letters. "Yes?"

"Have there been any applicants for the singing instructor's position?" Christine kept her tone light and unconcerned.

"There have been a few, but none that I would consider to be qualified." Madame matched Christine's tone, though Christine thought she spied a twitch to Madame's lips.

Christine glanced back to the stage and thought, *why not?* If she started exercising her voice now, she would be prepared to take on the position when the school opened. To share her gift of song with others was an exhilarating idea. To teach the grace and beauty of opera and watch her passion unfold before her very eyes... Christine's heart began to pound. *This is what Erik must have felt when he tutored me. How he encouraged me and enriched my life...* Christine faltered at the memory; perhaps this was not such a splendid idea after all.

Madame Giry leaned away from her desk and gazed at Christine from across the room. "If not you, Christine, then who?"

Christine gave a jerky nod and took in a trembling breath. She ascended the steps to the stage and started to practice her scales. Her throat soon loosened, and she sang an uncomplicated ballad. Madame Giry stopped her work to listen, a pleased smile on her face. Christine felt her own face relax with the delight and ease of her music. How wonderful to sing just for the enjoyment of it!

As she reached the song's conclusion, Christine decided to end it with a flourish. She opened her mouth, letting the notes climb higher and higher. When she finished, she clasped her hands to her heart and wept soundless tears of joy. She had indeed forgotten this part of her soul, but she would never make that mistake again, no matter whom she loved.

"Brava." The sound of light clapping came from the doorway. Madame Giry rose so fast she almost knocked her chair over.

Christine's heart stopped. "E-Erik?"

"I am afraid not, Vicomtesse." Ducray strolled into the school after shutting the doors behind him and executed a bow. "Your voice is superb."

"Her name is Christine. And what are you doing here?" Irate, Madame marched to Ducray and waited for an answer.

To Christine's amusement, the distinguished man became quite flustered. A touch of red stained his neck from underneath his starched white collar, and perhaps for the first time in his life, he stammered as he looked at Madame. "Christine...I see...that is..." Ducray shot an impatient look over to the stage, with a tightlipped incline of his head, he murmured, "Christine, my apologies."

Christine bestowed a grateful smile on him. Madame still glared. "Thank you, Ducray. No more of this Vicomtesse nonsense. The poor girl has dealt with enough. Now where has your master been hiding? There is still work to be done."

At that comment, Ducray pulled himself together and resumed his haughty butler persona. "My lord will not return to this school. Ever. He did send me to inquire if you need anything in the way of supplies or money." Ducray glanced over to Christine and then back to Madame Giry. In an undertone that nevertheless reached Christine's ears he inquired, "Did you receive my last letter, little flower?"

Now it was Madame who turned pink. She drew her small frame up most impressively and gave Ducray a scathing look. "I don't know what you mean, monsieur. And I will thank you not refer to me as an object with silly, fragile petals."

Ducray had the audacity to wink at her. "It is not the petals that remind me of you. It is the sturdy stem that supports the beautiful face."

Christine stifled the urge to laugh as Madame's embarrassment shifted to confusion. She could almost hear Madame wondering if she had been insulted, and was surprised when Madame chose to ignore Ducray's comments and address the problem of Erik's refusal to return. "I have sent him a note only this morning. Could you ask that he responds in person?"

"For you, Madame Giry, I would do that and more."

"It is a simple request, Ducray. Please ask him. I require nothing more."

Ducray smiled and bowed deeply to Madame. "As you wish, Mademoiselle Giry. I am at your disposal."

Madame scowled at his retreating form. "If only that were true, I would indeed dispose of you, Ducray." Her words hit their mark; Ducray's walk took on an agitated gait as he strode out the doors.

Flushed with victory, Madame whirled around so that she faced Christine, unaware that she beamed. Christine stood on the stage staring at her with open-mouthed shock.

Madame arched her eyebrow in challenge. "Yes, Christine? You have something you wish to say?"

With a sense of self-preservation, Christine started her scales again and Madame Giry returned to her work.

"Well, Ducray?" Erik sat, a solitary figure at the vast dining room table, eating his supper alone. He dug into his seasoned asparagus as if it were his only concern.

"Madame Giry wishes that you respond to her note in person."

Erik enjoyed the slight flavor of rosemary on his tongue before swallowing his bite. "That will not happen." He picked up a glass of rich, burgundy wine and swirled it in smooth motions. "And the other? Has she ceased her cleaning and run home to her darling husband?"

"No, my lord." Ducray watched as the wine glass paused in its movement. "She has not run home, nor does she clean."

"Ducray, out with it. I find that I cannot banter when it comes to this particular subject."

"She was singing, my lord."

The swirling halted. "Christine was singing?"

"With all her heart, my lord."

Erik drained the glass of its contents. *What did this mean? Why was she intent on surprising him at every turn just when he thought he had her figured out?* "I will be visiting the school tomorrow."

"Her voice is incomparable."

"Yes, Ducray, I know this beyond reason."

Chapter 23

UNDER strict orders to ready the Vicomtesse's chamber every night, Simone clucked her tongue in disapproval as she folded back the bedcovers in a clean line. The Vicomtesse would not be sleeping in this bed tonight or any other night.

But if the Vicomte were to return from the bright parties of Paris and see that his orders were not carried out, Simone knew that this time she would be released from her employment. Dismissed for not smoothing pillows of the runaway Vicomtesse—what would happen if the Vicomte only knew he still employed the very reason his wife's disappearing act had been a success?

Erik watched Christine sing from the dim confines of his office at the school, which afforded a clear view of her on stage while allowing him to remain hidden. It seemed his entire life had consisted of this, watching her from the darkness, loving her from a distance. And he loved her even now, he loved her without hope. As many times as he had lay open his heart, she either could not or would not say the words that he would give his life, no, that he would give up his music, to hear. His simple heart only knew his pure love for Christine, and his brilliant mind could not argue with such purity, no matter how badly it wounded.

She had finished her practice scales and began to sing; Erik closed his eyes and inhaled the splendor of her voice. His soul rejoiced; he had taught her this. The beast had brought beauty into this world.

He drank in the sight of her standing up on that stage, eyes bright, her shining spirit infusing every note that came out of her mouth with radiance. He had nurtured and cultivated the song inside of Christine until it had melded with every part of her being. And now she wished to share it with others, and that had always been Erik's dream as well. He allowed himself the pleasure of her voice until the song reached its conclusion.

His heart weighted, Erik placed a half mask over his face and stepped from the shadows. "Excellent, Christine. Your voice has not suffered from lack of use."

Christine's hand darted to her throat and she stared transfixed as he approached the stage. Madame Giry glanced up from her response letters in surprise and set her pen down to watch the exchange.

Erik reached the platform and looked up at Christine, his voice polite and even. "May I assume that you are looking to fill the singing instructor's position?"

Her wits scattered in the face of his unruffled demeanor. "Y-Yes," Christine croaked. She moistened her lips and tried again. "Yes, I was hoping to."

"And you feel that you are qualified?" Erik adjusted the sleeve of his jacket so that it aligned with his shirt cuff.

Feeling like a small, frayed ball of yarn being toyed with by a large, bored cat, Christine decided sincerity was her only option. "I had the very best of teachers."

The remark grabbed Erik's absolute attention, his gaze riveted upon her, and Christine saw in that gaze that she had severely hurt him with the reminder of a young girl and her cherished Angel.

"Erik...you gave me a gift that I can never repay."

His eyes shuttered then and there was nothing more to be read in the granite wall of his expression. He kept his tone clipped as he answered her. "See that you try. These students will be paying a handsome sum to attend this school."

"Of course I will do my best!"

Christine's chin tilted up a fraction of an inch, and Erik arched a brow at her. "And how long will this last? I cannot run a school wondering if the righteous Vicomte is going to come galloping up, yelling his arrogant head off, brandishing a sword and terrifying my students."

"You needn't worry about that. He does not know where I am." She crouched down on the stage so that she and Erik were at eye level. "I have left him." Perhaps her own wistful imagination saw the hitch of his breath as his sharp eyes darted to her unadorned ring finger and then back to her face.

"Very well, the position is yours." Something cold and unfriendly lurked in his tone as he added, "When you have changed your mind yet again and return to your husband, please give Madame ample notice so she may find a replacement. If you will excuse me?" He quit her presence before she could reply.

Disconcerted, Christine looked to Madame Giry, who merely pursed her lips and shook her head in exasperation.

Madame reread the response she had written to one of the applicant's parents.

> *Dear Monsieur and Mademoiselle Blanchard,*
>
> *We are pleased to inform you that your son, Henri, has been accepted at the École de musique Gustof-Daaé.*
>
> *Please do not concern yourself with the lack of funds to pay for his tuition.*
>
> *It will be taken care of by the Earl of Chester, as will the gift of a new violin.*
>
> *We thank you for contacting us and will be providing a tutoring schedule two weeks prior to the school's opening.*
>
> *Sincerely,*
> *Madame Giry, Headmistress*

⇀

Rumors of his wife's illness had taken on a life of their own. According to society, the Vicomtesse was not long for this world. Rather amazed, Raoul could count on one hand the number of times that he had vaguely mentioned Christine being ill. Now he was besieged with sympathetic wishes from his friends and speculative gazes from mothers who made sure that their eligible princesses made the acquaintance of the soon-to-be-widowed Vicomte.

At times Raoul almost believed it himself. His disastrous marriage seemed like a chaotic life that belonged to someone he once knew. He enjoyed the fawning attention, the admiration and respect that polite society lavished upon him. When he relaxed at his gentlemen's club, as he did now, sipping on perfectly aged port, or when he led some young debutante about the dance floor, he found it so easy to believe that this was his life and that nothing unpleasant had interrupted the well-oiled hinges of his existence. The ailing wife about whom everyone whispered, became only a hazy speck of difficulty, which Raoul chose to blithely ignore. He wanted badly to believe he was indeed the tragic figure that society's brush painted him.

Yet, no matter how strongly he affected his deliberate blindness, the truth slammed his lids open, forcing him to see, causing himself to be submersed once more in the boiling emotions of betrayal and fury. Christine rejected the life he had given her, the love he had given her. He could not pinpoint when it had started, but Christine had also been looking at him as if she found him completely lacking of worth, or as if *he* were the villain in these depraved circumstances.

Even worse, when he forced himself to look in the mirror, he saw the exact same thing he'd seen in Christine's eyes. Raoul had begun to recoil from mirrors. He took a deep swallow of the liquor to loosen his taut nerves.

His glass now emptied, Raoul stood up and decided to try his luck at cards. Christine could not hide forever, and while he waited, he would damn well enjoy himself. Yet, Madame's words taunted him. *"What will you do with your runaway Vicomtesse, my lord? What will you do with a woman who does not love you anymore?"*

With supreme effort, he managed to suppress the one startling consideration that came to mind. Life would be simpler if he never had to find out.

Christine spent the next few days alternating between basking in the undisguised admiration of Erik as he dropped whatever task he was engaged in to listen while she practiced her vocals, and then plunging into melancholy when he resumed ignoring her the moment she finished.

She had made several pathetic attempts to talk to him about the school, if only to be near him for a moment. The invariable answer always came, curt and dismissive. "Please discuss any school related issues with Madame Giry."

Madame, at her wits end with Christine's naiveté, did not bother to shield the younger woman from her frustration. "Why are you doing this to him?" she demanded.

"I don't know what you mean." Christine was taken aback by Madame's abrasive question.

"Christine, he has allowed you to reopen the school. He tortures himself these past days listening to you sing because he cannot deny himself. He wants your love, and you come to him with talk of compositions."

"He will reject me."

"Then give him that chance! Just as he gave it to you so many times." Madame sighed and smoothed her hand over Christine's curls. "He deserves that."

Christine thought of the man who played up in his tower. She could picture Erik's long, sensitive fingers crashing down on the keys as he strove to express the churning currents of his spirit. The notes that would roll and thunder down the stairway always left her breathless and aching. She was as captive to his song as he was to hers. The school could have tumbled down about her head and she would never notice while Erik's melody enraptured.

"You are right as always, Madame. But he deserves more than this sad little creature that I have become, and he deserves more then my belated offering of love as well."

"Be that as it may, Christine, it is your love and your love alone that he wants." When Christine did not respond, Madame gestured toward the doors. "We have a long day ahead of us tomorrow. We should go now."

Haunting, powerful music reached their ears. Christine gazed at the winding staircase, feeling a pull so strong she took two steps before she became of aware of moving.

"Go to him, Christine." Madame Giry grabbed Christine's hands between her own. "Listen to your heart, listen to his music…you will find that the melody is the same."

Blind panic blocked out the accuracy of Madame's words. "No, no…if I do that then I have nothing left!"

"What are you saying, Christine? If you go up those stairs you have everything." Madame released Christine's hand and stared at the anxious young girl with frustration.

Christine would not be swayed. "If he throws the words back in my face, I cannot pretend any longer. I will know that I have hurt him beyond repair and that he will never return my love. I choose to leave things as they are. I will sing for him on that stage every day for the rest of my life if that is the only time I know that I can bring him happiness. Besides," Christine added with regret, "I cannot offer what is not mine to give. Raoul will never divorce me."

Madame let Christine go and retrieved her cloak without saying another word. Sometimes all the words in the world were not enough.

As the waltz ended, Raoul brought his lovely partner to a stop with a flourish. The girl smiled demurely and accepted his proffered arm. They made a charming couple, and many people were quick to gossip that the Vicomte had waltzed with her only just last night at another ball.

Raoul led the girl back to her beaming mother, but before she could she start to list her daughter's attributes, a carrying voice called out to Raoul.

"Vicomte de Chagny!" A tall woman excitedly beckoned Raoul to her side.

Raoul smiled at the Comtesse Leroux and excused himself from his present company, much to the mother's dismay.

"Comtesse, you look lovely this evening." Raoul bent low over her hand and kissed the air above it.

The older woman simpered, her heavily rouged face creasing into smiles. "Vicomte, it is always a lovely evening when you loan us your presence." The Comtesse scanned the crowded ballroom. "Ah, there he is."

At Raoul's quizzical look, the Comtesse smiled triumphantly. "I have an old friend who has just returned from the country. He knows of the Earl of Chester's family."

"Indeed?" Raoul said, intrigued. Discovering the identity of the Earl had become something of a game throughout Parisian society.

As the Earl's power increased, so did his mystery. The aristocrats were mad for any information involving the Elusive Earl, or E.E., to which he was now referred.

The Earl was an unseen force to be reckoned with.

Raoul's mind tugged on a distant, locked away memory. This Earl and the mystery that cloaked him seemed so familiar all of a sudden.

An elderly gentleman made his way toward them. When he joined them, the Comtesse tucked her arm cozily through his. "Francois, so good to see you! Please tell us all you can about the Elusive Earl. We are just dying to know."

―――

Earlier that day, the irritable state of Erik's disposition had churned into a full-blown temper when he discovered that Christine and Madame Giry had been traveling alone. He left the school without saying a word and returned late in the afternoon with an enclosed carriage, a team of horses, and a burly man who would serve as both driver and protector.

He still could not bring himself to speak to the women. After showing them their new means of transport, Christine had the audacity to thank him for the conveyance as if it were a pleasant surprise.

"That was so thoughtful of you, Erik."

Madame Giry smiled her agreement.

Anger returned at their unconcerned complacency. Did they not understand the peril of traveling alone? And now they stood here smiling and thanking him when they should be on their knees thanking *God* they had not been attacked.

He emitted a low growl in the back of his throat and pushed past the startled women. Again, he sought refuge in his tower room. As he climbed the stairs, he tortured himself with images of Christine bleeding and broken in the streets. And Madame Giry! He once credited her with an immeasurable amount of common sense; apparently his appraisal of everyone's character was badly skewed. Erik reached the top of the landing and crossed over to his pipe organ, his sanity.

Hours passed as he ran his fingers over the smooth keys and let his mind drift and wander. He knew he could not be near Christine much longer without breaking down. Erik could envision an eternity of offering his heart only to be met with that sad look of apology as she refused to accept it. That look nearly killed him once, and it would have succeeded that time at his home if he had been the same creature from the Opera House. If he hadn't met the old Earl who'd taught him the value of himself and the meaning of love, Erik would have never have survived these encounters with Christine that carved a deeper void into his heart, slice by agonizing slice.

He stopped playing as he reflected on his friendship with the Earl. Perhaps it was time to take that voyage to America. They had discussed it on more than one occasion. Erik recalled the Earl's hopeful voice as he spoke of all the exciting things he wished to experience in the new world. But he never added it to his list of things to see. Erik decided at that moment he would honor his friend's memory with this trip and in so doing, guard his soul from Christine.

He would begin preparations tonight and be on his way tomorrow.

The Comtesse made brief introductions between Francois and Raoul. The old man looked fondly at the Comtesse. "I do not have much information, my dear Claudette. Your father must be laughing in his grave to see me gossiping at a ball."

Claudette giggled, a sound much out of place from a woman of her years. "Father was a stick in the mud, and you have always had a soft spot for me. So, I demand you gossip!"

Raoul found himself leaning toward Francois, the blood coursing faster through his veins.

Francois puffed out his narrow chest and cleared his throat. "Really, there is not much to tell. The Earl of Chester is an old title. The family was once quite prominent in society until the past sixty years or so. That's when things become murky. I know the Earl and Countess had a son. He was an only child. I do not know if he married or if any other children have been born to this line. What is strange though, is this sudden flurry of activity. By all accounts, if the son had no children, he would be of advanced years, and I can't imagine where the sudden interest in power would come from." Francois shrugged.

"I am an old man myself, and I tell you the last thing I think of when I can get myself out of bed in the morning is helping the needy and funding politics."

The Comtesse looked crestfallen, but then brightened. "Perhaps the old Earl did have a son!" She looked slyly at Raoul. "A rich, mysterious, bachelor of a son. Ooh, isn't that a delicious thought. You had better watch out, Vicomte!"

Raoul paid no attention to the Comtesse; he kept his eyes on Francois. He saw something else in the old man's face, some last piece of information that he dreaded intuitively. Francois furrowed his brow. *What is it, man? What tale does that musty relic of a mind search for?*

Francois's brow cleared and he smiled. "There is one other thing. I cannot understand why I did not remember this to begin with."

"Tell, tell!" The Comtesse's eyes gleamed with the excitement of exclusive tittle-tattle.

"He was deformed. The heir to the Earldom was born with half his face so disfigured he was forced to wear a mask from birth. The parents hid him away until their deaths, and no one has seen or heard from him until now."

A mask. As soon as the words came out of the old man's mouth, the blinders fell from Raoul's eyes. He had been searching for an Opera Ghost, but somehow the demon had metamorphosed into an Earl. The jagged fragments that hovered on the edges of Raoul's subconscious snapped together with perfect clarity. It felt like a hundred archers launched their pointed arrows at him as each memory lanced through his brain.

The timing of it all, the notes, the manipulations, the school… Raoul felt a murderous rage rush up from the blackest pit of his soul. It engulfed him, it fed him and when he rushed out of the ballroom, it reminded him that he would need his sword before riding to his destination: the *École de musique Gustof-Daaé*.

Chapter 24

"CHRISTINE, he is not coming down. Why not wait until his anger has abated? Speak with him tomorrow." Madame folded the last of her letters into its envelope and rolled her shoulders, stretching out her muscles. "I cannot fault Erik for his condemnation of our behavior, but I am unaccustomed to answering to anyone and unaccustomed to feeling foolish. Now, I am tired and on edge, and I want to go home."

The pipe organ had ceased its music, and the silence filled Christine's heart with a strange melancholy. She glanced toward the stairs time after time, waiting to hear Erik's footsteps. Something about the word tomorrow seemed empty and untrue. It lacked its usual promise of what could be. Christine wondered at this sense of foreboding.

"I am going to ask him to accompany us home. He will not argue the need for added protection against unseen threats in the night."

Both women looked out a nearby window to the absolute darkness outside. The air around them shifted and grew suddenly chill.

Not a superstitious woman by nature, Christine was taken aback when Madame grabbed Erik's cloak and walking stick and thrust them at Christine. "Hurry." The abrupt word carried the same sense of urgency that tightened Christine's nerves.

"Christine!"

The women jumped in unison and exhaled in relief when they saw Erik standing at the bottom of the steps, scowling at the sight of Christine holding his belongings. "May I ask what you are doing?"

Christine clutched the items against her defensively. "I was about to ask if you would be kind enough to escort us home."

"Escort you home?" Erik echoed in puzzlement, "Why? You have been escorting yourselves home without anyone, and now I have provided you with ample security."

"I am afraid." She admitted, and a warm flush crept up her cheeks. "Though I do not know why."

Christine felt an overpowering need to memorize the compelling landscape of Erik's face. When he stepped closer to her, she hoped he could read the earnest truth in her wide gaze.

But he simply retrieved his things from her grasp. "Very well, I shall accompany the two of you in the carriage. I have some news that I wish to share at any rate."

"Does it involve the school?" Madame asked in a wary tone.

Erik did not answer; he laid his walking stick against Madame's desk and started to don his cloak.

"You are leaving." Christine said, her voice barely above a whisper.

Erik shook his head in resignation, put his cloak down and faced Christine. "Yes. I am traveling to America. I have fulfilled my obligations to the school and will leave it in your capable hands."

Madame Giry nodded her head as if she had expected this terrible news.

Christine grabbed his cloak from the desk and clutched it against her as if that could prevent his leaving. "No! You cannot leave!" Her voice rose, shrill and desperate.

"Why? There is nothing more to keep me." Though Erik's tone cut, his eyes begged her to say otherwise.

Christine struggled against the chains of her own fears and lost. "There is still so much to do here."

And just like that, she witnessed the light of Erik's soul die. He gazed silently at Christine and only the solitary tear that slid from underneath the mask betrayed his pain.

From instinct, Christine reached up to brush away the tear. Madame Giry stopped her with a sharp, reproachful, "No," and pulled Christine's hand away.

"Fiend!" The doors flew open and Raoul strode inside the school, his sword held at the ready.

Madame gasped and grabbed Christine to her side. To their horror, Erik did not move as Raoul stalked toward him.

An unholy glow emanated from Raoul's eyes when his sword made its first shallow cut.

Christine screamed as a long blossom of crimson spread across the white fabric of Erik's shirt. Still he did not move.

With Raoul's second slash, Erik flinched and stumbled back a few steps.

Christine tried to pull away from Madame's tight grasp. "You will get yourself killed, Christine," she hissed. "Or you will get him killed faster for your interference."

Raoul smiled in satisfaction as the first wound began to drip. "So the monster does not fight. Perhaps you finally realize that I am doing the world a favor by ridding it of your repulsive existence."

Two more slices followed. Raoul kept the cuts trivial, as though he wanted to draw out each moment of Erik's suffering. He took no pains to hide the immense pleasure he felt as his sword cut into the Opera Ghost's flesh.

By the time Raoul's slashes had pushed Erik up against Madame's desk, little white remained on the front of Erik's saturated, bloody shirt. Red droplets splattered across the school papers.

"For God sake, Erik, fight him!"

Raoul's head whipped around to stare at Christine. Bile rose until he could taste it in the back of his throat. She wanted her hideous lover to fight her husband…her husband!

He turned his attention back to his enemy and aimed the sword at Erik's stomach. "It is time to end this. I doubt you have a heart inside that miserable carcass, so I will have to be content with cutting out your rotten insides."

Erik's breath came in shallow pants. He allowed himself one final look at the woman he prized above all else before he closed his eyes and braced himself.

Raoul drew the sword back slightly.

"I love you!" The three words burst from Christine with more power than any aria she had ever sung. "Erik, I love you."

Erik's eyes flew open, and Raoul's stunned gaze flew back to Christine, though his sword remained poised.

Madame Giry reached in her pocket and drew out a set of polished rosary beads. She clasped them in front of her as the younger woman stepped toward the two men. Christine had eyes only for Erik, but directed her words at Raoul.

"I love him now at his best…and I loved him then at his worst. It will always be Erik… I am so very sorry, Raoul."

Madame drew in a swift breath of astonishment.

Erik slowly straightened, disbelief and wonder etched in his face.

Raoul trembled with the force of his wrath. "Sorry, Christine? Allow me to show you what sorry means! This is farewell to your Phantom."

Erik slapped the flat of the blade away from his stomach, knocking the sword from Raoul's grasp. In a flash of movement, he grabbed his walking stick and unsheathed a long, thin rapier. Raoul scrambled to his own weapon and picked it up in time to parry Erik's first violent thrust.

And so it began. Both skilled with their weapons and filled with resolution the clash of steel rang throughout the school time and time again. As Erik easily deflected Raoul's sword once more, Raoul took up a feral offensive position, frenzied in his determination to win this grim battle.

Soon the Vicomte's strategy became more erratic, his swordplay less controlled. Expressionless, Erik parried each attack until the fight moved dangerously close to Christine and Madame. Frantic to shield them, Erik tried to position himself in between Raoul's reckless blade and the women. His effort came too late; Raoul lunged at Erik, sweeping his blade in a wild arc. As the tip of the sword sliced through the skin of her forearm, Christine cried out in agony.

Erik roared his fury and shoved Raoul back with brutish strength. Raoul's sword, jarred from his grip, skittered across the marble floor.

Now Raoul faced the Opera Ghost without defenses. He backed away from the steady slash of Erik's rapier, but his retreat mattered not; Erik refused to yield in his pursuit, shredding Raoul's clothing, leaving as many gashes of crimson in his blade's wake as he'd collected from the other man.

Madame tended to Christine's laceration with a piece of cloth torn from her skirt to stop the sluggish bleeding.

"I know it is painful, but at least the wound is a superficial one."

Christine suffered a far greater agony as she watched the battle. She did not wish for Raoul's death; she did not want Erik to kill.

Madame wrapped a bandage around Christine's arm and squeezed her hand. "You have given him your love; make sure that your faith in him comes with it."

Across the room, Raoul ceased his retreat; he looked at Erik with steady acceptance. "Just end it, then."

His sword arm raised in the air, Erik hesitated, then lowered the blade and narrowed his eyes. "I never intended to kill you, Vicomte." He quirked his lips as if to imply Raoul's life were of little value to him.

Raoul clenched his jaw and jerked his head in the direction of Christine. "For her?" he asked with derision.

Erik rested the tip of his sword on the ground. "No. For myself."

Raoul sneered at Erik as if he could not fathom a creature such as him possessing integrity.

"However, this is for her." Erik swiftly closed the distance between them and wrapped his large hand around Raoul's throat. He held Raoul that way until he had him shoved up against the wall. Raoul's attempts to push back were as futile as trying to outwit fate.

As he struggled to escape the crushing grip, his face took on a mottled shade of purple.

"Do I have your attention?" Erik inquired baldly. He loosened his hold only enough to ensure that Raoul listened.

His dark voice grew even darker still as he continued, "I know hell, Vicomte. I know its complexities and its devastation. If you do not heed this most sincere advice, that will be the world I bring down on your head. I am the Earl of Chester now; the Opera Ghost is no more. The men who owe me favors or money are amongst the most influential in this country. There are no damsels in distress that need rescuing from a monster. Christine is mine. She has made her choice. Share your lifetime with someone else or live in wretched solitude; either way, do not interfere in our lives again. Are we understood?"

Raoul glared at Erik. Even now he would not back down, but Erik knew that his message penetrated far deeper than any sword thrust.

He released the Vicomte and stepped away; his other hand never loosening its grip on the hilt of his rapier.

Raoul pulled himself from the wall and staggered toward the open doors. He rasped out Christine's name.

When she met his gaze solemnly, he flinched at something he saw in her wounded eyes. "I have always loved you, Little Lotte. I loved you at your best, and I love you now at your worst." His eyes focused on her bandage. "I never meant to hurt you."

Both knew he referred to more than her wound.

Christine's voice was laden with sorrow. "I know, Raoul. Nor did I."

But if Raoul gained a measure of ease from her response, he did not show it. He stumbled out the open doors, and the darkness swallowed him.

"Well," Madame said briskly, "we will need to clean those wounds, Monsieur Erik. Christine and I will bring some cloth and ointment to your room. Christine, come with me."

Surprised at Madame's abrupt request, Christine wavered. She needed to be with Erik right now. "But Madame Giry…" Christine looked uncertainly over to Erik who still stared out the doorway into the night beyond. He did not glance her way.

With a sigh, she reluctantly followed Madame to a supply closet, gathered the necessary supplies, and then traveled down a short hallway into the windowless room where Erik slept when he played long past midnight.

Vibrant tapestries hung on the stone walls, depicting various opera's played out onstage. A thick woven carpet covered most of the rough wooden planks of the floor. Only two items of furniture graced the room: a large four-poster bed, a table that held a washbasin, and a porcelain vase of long-stemmed red roses. A squat coal-burning stove sat in the corner, casting a dim, rosy glow about the room.

Christine checked the water in the basin to make sure it was clean. Madame Giry handed her the cloths and ointment. As she placed the items on the washbasin, Christine stared at her own hands, seeing for the first time how they shook.

Madame leaned over and inhaled the scent of Erik's roses. "The man has faultless taste when it comes to beauty." She tilted her head and looked at Christine.

Her gaze contained concern and was tinged with a touch of challenge. "Much has happened this eve; so many things have been brought to the light. It is much for a girl to take in. So I ask you, *Mignonne*, is it I who shall tend to Erik's wounds?"

Though shaken to the core in the aftermath of the evening's ordeal, Christine let the freedom inside her heart overrule any hesitation. "No, Madame Giry. I will tend to Erik."

Madame Giry smiled softly at the young woman in front of her. She kissed her fingertips and touched them to Christine's forehead. "As it should be. A great deal needs to be healed between the two of you. I will send him in."

Christine's heart pounded at the image of her and Erik alone together, without discord, without masks. "Madame, may I request a favor?"

"Of course, Christine. What is it?"

Christine selected one of the roses from the vase and handed it to Madame. "Please give this to Erik and tell him it will be the last time he will ever have to come to me."

Chapter 25

UNSURE of what to do with herself while she waited for Erik to appear, Christine sat atop the only piece of furniture available, Erik's bed. She ran her hand across the lush material of his bedspread, and a sinuous shiver trickled down her spine. Yet another extension of the man himself, the bedding thrilled, invited, and tantalized.

Everything about Erik beguiled the senses. Christine recalled the crisp texture of his linen shirt underneath her cheek, along with the faint tang of his cologne each time he held her in his arms. She thought of the strong column of his neck, his skin so warm to the touch, the steady pulse that beat just below the corded muscle. His music, a pagan seduction that ignited her soul and made her want...

"I never thought to receive a rose from you."

"Erik!" Christine rose quickly from the bed.

He remained in the doorway, hesitation written on his face.

A shy smile played on Christine's lips, making it clear that they both were nervous, but inviting him in regardless.

He crossed to her and stopped, filling the room and her senses with his vital presence. Erik tilted her chin so he could look into her eyes. "I never thought to be gifted with your heart." He spoke again, his voice husky with suppressed emotion. "Christine, I—"

She cut him off with a shake of her head. "Allow me the honor of saying it first, of saying it always." Christine placed her hands on Erik's shoulders, stood up on her toes and kissed his mouth. "I love you, Erik." She stared into the stormy depths of his eyes and sighed, "Dear god, how I love you so," and kissed him again.

As she made to pull back, Erik held her fast refusing to allow too much space between them. Christine thrilled in response of his ardor; but still she maintained some distance in order to keep her mind clear for what she had to say. "Erik, my thoughts are too scattered being so close to you and my heart insists that I tell you this now."

Erik's arms loosened their hold and Christine stepped back, holding his hands. "I cannot change the past, but I can offer you the present and future of my love if you will have it…if you will have me." She faltered and looked away from his intent gaze, her tears hot and swift, her words simple and true. "I love you, and I am sorry to have hurt you so many times."

"Christine, am I so perfect then? You have never once denied forgiveness of me, and surely if there is anyone that should be pleading for exoneration, it is I. We have made our mistakes and have paid for them." He held her face in his hands, wiping away the path of tears with his thumbs. "No more sorrow, Christine. We have no room for that any longer. Now is our time for happiness."

Hope filled her eyes. "Do we dare?" she whispered.

Erik let out a quiet laugh. Though he sought to hide it from her, she saw his slight wince.

"We should clean those cuts before they become infected," Christine murmured.

Erik paused. "I can take care of it myself if you would prefer. I will need to remove my shirt."

Christine glanced to the small stove, wondering. Had Madame added more coal before she left? The room had warmed. He must hear her heart pounding. She'd never known a desire this deep. She felt it flow into her veins, her limbs, her heart and welcomed its exhilarating presence. Only Erik would ever affect her so.

"I want to do this for you. If you would just sit down you will make it easier for me to tend to you." She heard the fall of his shirt on the floor as she dampened some of the cloths and was sorely tempted to lay one of the cool squares against her forehead.

She turned around. Erik stood in his dark breeches; mask still in place, bloody slashes crisscrossing his upper torso in violent streaks. Christine reached for him with the cloth in hand when a flash of sparkle caught her eye. She dropped the cloth and faltered toward Erik, unable to believe what her mind told her she had seen.

"This is my ring?" Christine slid her finger up under the chain so that the bit of jewelry rested in her palm. She looked up at Erik in astonishment. "You have worn it all this time?"

"I have worn it since the day you brought it back to me—worn it with two different sentiments." Erik's voice was solemn. "One was anger…I wore it to remind myself of your rejection."

Christine shook her head vehemently. "No, that is not why—"

"Sssshh." Erik tucked Christine's fingers around the ring with a gentle caress and held his hand over hers. "I later wore the ring to bring me faith… that perhaps someday you would love me."

"That night in the lair, I needed to let you know what was in my heart, though I couldn't be with you. My love was there, Erik, only I feared you more." Remorse clouded her voice. "I thought I understood everything so clearly."

"You loved the last fragment of humanity in my soul that night. But had you stayed, I would have eventually killed yours."

Christine did not know whether she needed to purge herself of the guilt she carried or have Erik heap more on her shoulders as she voiced her terrible confession. "But…I left with Raoul. I thought I loved him as well. You have always been so certain of your heart, and I have been so confused with mine."

"Christine, I never thought a day would come that I would be thankful you made the choice you did. You saved both our souls, and that action brought us to this place, to this night. And I cannot lament a past that has restored my soul and brought you back to me."

Erik slipped the chain over his head and let it slide from his hand onto the bed. "I do not need to wear the ring any longer. However, I think we shall keep it as a reminder of faith and love."

Taking Erik's hand, Christine laid it against her heart. "I am no longer confused." She noticed one of Erik's cuts had oozed a few tiny beads of blood.

"Oh Erik, I'm sorry—I was supposed to be attending to your injuries!" She hurried to the table and grabbed another damp cloth, then stopped short when she faced him again. The ring had distracted her from truly taking in the vision of Erik.

He grimaced. "I am afraid I am not an appealing sight."

But Christine saw only the sculpted perfection of Erik's form, and she could not speak.

"Christine?"

"You are beautiful."

"Beautiful," Erik repeated, his eyes vulnerable. "A word I had not thought possible to apply to me. Yet, as I stand before you and you gaze at me in such a manner, I think it is possible…that I could be beautiful."

He held himself still as Christine rested the cloth over the muscled expanse of his chest. The white material created a sharp contrast to his dark skin. With infinite care and concentration, Christine swabbed away most of the dried blood. "I think the gods could not accept a mere mortal possessing such beauty within and without. I think that is why your face needed to be flawed. Only you have had the last laugh; you have turned that supposed flaw into your greatest strength."

He stared down at Christine in awe. "How is it that you have always seen past the beast?"

Christine stopped her ministrations and looked back at him, her eyes soft and compelling. "How is it that you have always seen past the scared little girl and into my woman's soul?"

She returned to the table to retrieve a fresh cloth. Erik sucked in his breath as she ran the soft cotton tenderly over the cuts on his abdomen, wiping away the last of the blood.

"Did I hurt you?" Christine left her hand resting on his stomach, too mesmerized by the feel of his body to pull away.

"No." Erik answered quietly. "But I think. . . that is enough." He clenched his hands by his sides.

Her breathing unsteady, Christine took Erik's hand and led him to the bed. "I still need to apply the ointment."

He sat down on the edge of the bed. "Christine." Warning and promise pulsed within two syllables.

"I know what I am doing." Christine leaned in to spread the salve over the first wound.

Erik's eyes flared. "Do you?"

She moved onto the next cut and whispered in his ear. "Yes, I do."

"Put down the ointment, Christine."

She let the small tin drop to the floor.

Erik stood, bringing Christine with him. She felt the heat of his hands through her dress as he held her. "Do you comprehend what you are saying?" he demanded. "If I take you into my bed, I will claim you heart, body and soul. There is no going back. No second thoughts."

Christine gave him a smile full of joy. "I love you." She stepped out of Erik's arms and slipped the pins from her hair. Her curls fell around her in tumbling disarray. "You have already claimed two of the three; if my body is the last thing I have to offer, then it is yours." She presented her back to him, pulling her hair aside to expose the long row of buttons on her dress. "All that I am is yours, Erik."

She could not see the passionate intensity that burned inside Erik's eyes, but she felt the slight tremor in his deft fingers as he slid each button out of its catch. Erik pushed the dress off of her shoulders; it pooled around Christine's ankles with a soft rustle. He placed his lips on the nape of her exposed neck, kissing her with soft heat.

Christine let her head fall back onto his shoulder. As his lips trailed a path of sweet, searing kisses to her ear and grazed the delicate lobe with his teeth, ribbons of pure desire coursed through her.

Erik held Christine against the length of his body, one hand rested on the flat of her stomach, while the other caressed the flare of her hip. "I will worship you this night and into forever." He swept her up in his arms and carried her to his bed. Tenderly, carefully, as if she were the most delicate of things, Erik laid Christine on the midnight blue coverlet. He drank in the sight of her, clad only in her ivory chemise, silk stockings and dainty slippers. His gaze lit on Christine's face, and she let him see inside of her, to her heart and all that she offered.

He regarded her for several long moments and then whispered, "I never thought to see you like this."

Christine blushed and looked down at her scant undergarments.

"I do not refer to your attire. I never dreamed that I would see the depth of my love for you mirrored in your eyes."

Erik walked over to the table.

Bewildered, Christine asked, "Erik?"

"Clear your mind, sweet Christine, and let the dream begin." He returned to the bed, one hand overflowing with rose petals. "Close your eyes."

Christine complied, letting darkness heighten her senses.

Erik took a petal and fluttered it across her eyelids. "This one is for the first time I gazed upon you."

Christine released a slow tremulous breath.

Erik took another petal and languidly ran its velvet texture over her mouth. "This one is for the first time you kissed me."

Christine's lips parted slightly, she could feel Erik's gaze resting on her mouth for a taut moment before he continued.

With a third sensuous petal he trailed it down the smooth skin of her neck. "This one is for the first time I heard you sing."

Molten heat flowed through her veins, thickening her blood; Christine touched her own neck, following the path of the rose petal.

With another petal, Erik drew slow circles over her heart. "And this one is for the first time you told me you loved me."

Christine opened her slumberous eyes. "And the others?"

Erik stood up and sprinkled the remaining petals over Christine and around the bed. She tilted her face up and enjoyed the sensation of the brief caresses to her skin as they floated down.

Erik joined her on the bed and covered Christine's body with his own, so that their hearts beat fiercely against each other. The intoxicating fragrance of the crushed petals surrounded them; Erik traced his finger around the oval of Christine's face. "The others are for tonight, and for the many other firsts that lie in our future."

"Another first then," Christine reached up and pulled off his mask, "No more barriers."

He gazed down at her, defenseless. "This is all that I am, Christine."

Christine set the mask aside and regarded Erik in wonder. "This is all, Erik? When I look at you, I cannot believe you are real—that such strength and splendor can exist in a mere mortal. God help me for I feel that I am not enough for you."

"Never." He kissed her then, and her heart sighed.

And as the night wore on both wandering souls at last found their way and laid claim to the other.

Chapter 26

AT some point in the early morning, Erik left her. Christine did not know what alerted her mind, or perhaps her heart, that Erik was gone from the bed.

Disoriented inside the windowless room, Christine still had a sense that the moon had only recently made her farewells. The coals glowed warmly in the stove; Erik must have thought to stoke the embers before leaving.

Though no sounds filled the school and no music reached her ears, Christine knew where she would find her missing Phantom; she just was not sure what she would find within him.

She climbed the twisting staircase until she reached the tower room. Erik sat on the polished wooden bench, facing away from his organ. In each hand he held one item: his mask and the ring. He stared at both with a disquieting intensity, as if by looking at them hard enough, he could solve whatever difficulty plagued him.

Christine then noticed a startling addition to the room; an enormous gilded mirror hung on the wall, opposite from where Erik sat. Angels and demons carved into the dull, gold frame with breathtaking yet disturbing craftsmanship. They frolicked and danced and copulated together. Though the demons were grotesque and the angels exquisite, it was obvious that they lived in decadent harmony. Christine's heart wrenched at the thought of Erik staring at and into this mirror while he played his brilliant music.

"It is only a mirror, Christine."

Christine gave a small gasp as Erik's voice broke into her musings. She turned to see his grim expression. Only hours ago light had danced in his eyes. Now that light burned dim and fixed.

She crossed to Erik, ignoring the invisible wall that he had erected, a forced smile set on her face. "You have to admit, much can be construed from its artwork."

"Last night should not have occurred." Erik's face was a mask of regret.

Christine's world spun dizzily for a moment and she felt the air whoosh from her lungs. She grasped the edge of the pipe organ to steady herself. "W-why are you saying this?"

A hazy shaft of sunlight caught the many facets of the ring as Erik twined the chain around his mask then placed it next to him on the bench. He gave it another long look before answering Christine. "We are not wed. I have done you a disservice of the lowest form because I was weak."

With no premeditation to the act, Christine's hand flew out and cracked with blazing accuracy across Erik's cheek. "How dare you!"

Erik touched his face in shock. His eyes were no longer dim, but glittered with hurt reprimand. Christine met his gaze with righteous anger. "How dare you take last night and turn it into a weakness of the flesh. You speak of marriage; last night was a marriage of our souls. Last night we spoke purer vows of love before each other, than most people speak before a priest. Last night I finally experienced all the bliss and pleasure that your eyes have promised for so long." Christine blinked away threatening tears in irritation. "And now…now you sit here and tell me that your flesh was weak. In one cruel sentence you crush the blessed happiness I have found in your arms into worthless rubble."

Erik shot up from the bench. "Enough!" he thundered. He looked into Christine's wounded countenance and closed his eyes as though he could not bear her suffering. "Enough, Christine," he pleaded softly.

"No, Erik…it will be enough when you take those hateful words back. I swear I will not let you leave this tower until you do so." Her small frame seemed to take on height with the force of her conviction. "I will not let you do this to us." Christine's voice caught in her throat and fear began to constrict her soul.

"Then do not let me." Suddenly his lips were on hers. He demanded all from her in that kiss, drinking deeply from the bottomless chalice of her conviction and love. Erik threaded his fingers through her hair and up her scalp. He buried his face in her neck, kissing her while murmuring fervent words of repentance.

He was a force of nature unto himself; Christine could not articulate the sensations that swept through her with the speed and strength of a hurricane. She had time only to note that Erik's lips covered hers again and she answered him with all the passion that only he could summon.

Erik crushed her against him. "I love you, I love you."

The words were a chant in place of endearment, and Christine worried what devil's curse he tried to ward off.

Then it came to her as her gaze caught on the reflection of their embracing forms. The thought held all the hushed clarity of a first snowfall and Christine stilled with her sudden understanding of this complex man.

She placed her hand on his bare chest, gentling him. "Erik, come with me."

Her heart broke a little when she saw the wary unease in his eyes. Christine prayed that her next actions would banish that wounded look forever.

She led him over to stand before the mirror, placing herself slightly in front of him, and drew his hand around her waist. They stared at their images. Erik's had immediately taken on a blank visage, while Christine regarded him closely, waiting.

"What is this about, Christine?" Erik asked, his voice guttural and sharp.

"What do you see, Erik?" Christine would not let him remove his hand from her waist. "Do not go yet. Please, tell me what you see."

Erik's face twisted in a mirthless grin. "I see an Angel and a Demon standing in front of a mirror. Is that what you wanted to hear?"

No, my love, that is the last thing I wanted to hear. God, give me the power to show him what I see through my eyes.

"You did not defile me, Erik. We did nothing wrong last night. There is nothing in this world that means more to me than the gift of yourself and your love. You are no demon, do you understand?"

If possible, Erik's features became even more remote. "Very well, I am not a demon. Can we move away from this godforsaken mirror now?"

One again Christine refused to let him pull away; if anything, she held on tighter. And she began to sing with quiet empathy. "Innocent child, you shall see me, know why in darkness I hide, gaze at yourself in the mirror—I wait there, inside…"

"Christine…" Erik's deep voice shook with fear and then, yearning.

Long ago, when the mask ruled the man, the Phantom had sung these very words in her dressing room, beckoning her from a mirror into his eternal world of midnight, veiling her eyes with music so enthralling she would never glimpse the monster that he saw himself to be.

Christine's song changed to her own verse. "Beautiful man in the mirror, I am inside you as well, we stand on the same side together—you have left your hell."

She hadn't taken her eyes off him in the mirror while she sang, and now she had to look away for a moment, afraid of what she might see. When she returned her gaze to Erik, Christine's breath caught in her throat. He smiled at her. That was all, a smile, but it came from a man whose distorted face never allowed for an existence involving the simple pleasure of this expression.

"Thank you." Again, such simplicity from him, yet the words held all the weight and worth of gold.

Christine turned and raised her face up to his. "No more talk of demons?"

His regard solemn, Erik cupped Christine's face within his hands. "I do not want to cause you pain; I wanted to save you from that… or perhaps I wanted to save myself. When I awoke this morning, I had almost hoped that I had dreamt it all, for the indescribable joy that filled me upon waking next to you terrified me in the next instant. And then I held your hand while you slept...and I was reminded of what it felt like to be a monster when I noticed the bareness of your finger where my ring should be. Always, when I have allowed myself the pleasure of envisioning a lifetime shared with you, I saw us as husband and wife. I have a title that I cannot even bestow upon you, as you so rightly deserve. These are the demons that pursue me now." Erik released her face with the last bitter sentence, his jaw set in an unforgiving line.

He will never make things easy on himself, Christine thought sadly.

She sighed and laced her fingers through his and smiled up at him. "It does not matter to me. We cannot have everything; I should think that love and happiness are enough."

Erik conceded her point with a short nod. "You would be right; I want nothing more than that as well. But what of Raoul? As long as the two of you are married, he will evermore be in our lives."

"He will not divorce. De Chagny's die before they divorce." The words came from nowhere; Christine had not understood what a profound imprint Raoul's statement had made. His careless comment had turned into a pulsing fear that lived in her head and threatened her newfound bliss. She would never seek divorce, nor would she show Erik how the memory rattled her. "It is of no importance. We will be happy."

She closed her eyes and kissed Erik, their mouths lingered, the experience still too new not to savor, too wonderful not to cherish. And if Erik disagreed with Christine's pronouncement, he did not show it by his actions. Christine left the tower room humming.

Erik grabbed the mask and the ring from the bench, then frowned as the ring pierced the skin of his palm, drawing a slight droplet of blood to the surface.

The flame in his eyes grew to fire. "You shall not have final say in our lives, Vicomte."

Chapter 27

THE bruised shadows underneath Christine's eyes that had been so prominent after her initial flight from Raoul had returned in the past days.

Madame looked across the table at her with concern as Christine aimlessly pushed around her coddled eggs.

"Christine, perhaps you should not go to the school today? You look unwell."

Christine glanced up in surprise, as if she had forgotten Madame's presence. "But we are so close to opening. I am fine, and if you could pass that on to Erik, I would be indebted."

Madame added a small amount of milk to her steaming cup of tea. "So, he is concerned as well? You have been pushing yourself too hard." Madame suspected that inner turmoil sapped the energy from Christine rather than the long hours she spent at the school. She stirred her tea in tiny, precise circles. "It must be hard, my dear, to have at last achieved your heart's desire only to discover large hurdles still loom. This past month has been a difficult one for you, *oui*?"

To Madame's astonishment Christine began weeping uncontrollably into her linen napkin. Madame got up from her seat and hurried over to comfort her young friend. "Christine, tell me what is wrong." Madame looked upward, seeking divine help, while she continued to hold Christine.

The tears subsided and Christine's breathing now came in bursts of hitched gasps. Madame pressed a cup of tea into her hand, which Christine accepted gratefully. She took several small sips and noticeably calmed. "Thank you, Madame. You always know what to do…or say for that matter. This past month has been wonderful and confusing. I had thought to be sharing Erik's home long before now. Thus far he keeps putting me off with excuses that he wants my rooms perfect, or that the house is not quite in order. What felt so right and pure that night has now started to take on a sordid tinge." Christine blushed and averted her eyes from Madame.

"I thought we had come to an understanding regarding marriage; it would seem that I was mistaken. But we cannot go on this way, living in separate homes yet wanting nothing more than to be with each other. I want a real life with him. I want to share each moment with him, as a husband and wife would do."

"And yet you are not husband and wife." Madame said the words in a matter-of-fact voice, then added in a gentler tone, "Don't you see Christine, while he may be able to understand that marriage is not possible, he will never accept it. His love for you will not allow anything, especially himself, to taint you. Erik's love demands perfection, demands that he honor you above all else, and I think he believes by taking you into his home or even by making love to you again, he is not true to his heart and therefore unworthy of yours."

Christine did not visibly react to Madame's plain speaking, except to fold her napkin and place it on the table next to her plate. "Then what are we to do? This is no life." She fell into a pensive silence.

Madame said nothing while she waited for Christine to work this problem out for herself. She returned to her seat and picked up her own cup of tea. As she began to drink, she caught a strange expression of fear that swept across Christine's features, though resolution replaced it within seconds. Madame was apprehensive to know Christine's thoughts.

Christine lifted her chin in stubborn decision. "I will talk to Raoul regarding a divorce."

"Do you think that it is wise? Your husband—" Christine flinched and Madame held up a placating hand, "The Vicomte, *oui*, he has been quiet. But one does not beard a wounded beast in his den.

His reactions are unpredictable. *Mon Dieu*, you had to escape from your own home, Christine. This idea of yours is very well to imagine, but to execute it would be reckless."

"Some place public, then? Madame, what other choice do I have? Once again, I am caught between two worlds. I need to end this, once and for all." Christine jumped up and braced her hands on the table as her eyes entreated Madame to see her point of view. "I see no other way. I—" Christine's face became washed of color; she swayed and gripped the edge of the table.

"Christine?"

Christine shook her head at Madame and ran from the table, down the hallway.

Madame found her in a spare bedroom retching emptily into a chamber pot.

"Oh, my dear." Madame crouched next to Christine and pulled her hair back away from her pale face.

The heaves abated, then finally stopped. Christine dragged herself into a sitting position and slumped against the wall.

Madame felt helpless for the first time in her life. A memory of Christine at seven years of age rose in Madame's mind. She closed her eyes and remembered the feel of Christine's small hand tucked so trustingly into her own on the day of Gustof Daae's death. Madame had done her best throughout Christine's life to guide her and love her; it hadn't been hard, Christine had become as much of a daughter to her as Meg was.

And now she had failed Christine, the daughter of her heart. "Christine." Madame moved next to her and smoothed a strand of dark hair on her forehead. "Christine, do you think you might be with child?" Madame's normally crisp voice faltered as she asked a question that should only bring joy when answered.

"Oh." Christine's gaze flitted about the room as if she searched for something lost. "Oh." She looked down at her hands resting in her lap and began to absently rub at her unadorned ring finger. The fear that had swept through her face earlier now returned and settled.

Madame grabbed Christine's hands to still them. "It will be

alright, *Mignonne*. I will be with you, the babe will be much loved. Erik will be such a proud papa. And now it is certain that Raoul will give you a divorce." She smiled earnestly at Christine, whose expression remained unchanged. "So you see Christine, you have nothing to fear."

"You do not understand, Madame." Christine tugged her hands from the older woman's comforting grasp, placed them back in her lap and stared straight ahead. The little color that had returned to her face drained with each word that she whispered. "I now have two reasons to speak with Raoul. Erik may not be the father."

Chapter 28

UPON seeing Christine enter the school, Erik immediately inquired if she felt any better. She went to him and paused an arm's length away, her normally expressive eyes frozen. Something about the way she held herself reminded him of a doe he had once seen caught in a hunter's snare. Entrapped himself, for years Erik was haunted by the fact he had been unable to save that helpless creature.

Her unsteady response, however soft, rang as clear as the peal of church bells in his ears. "I believe I am with child." Christine took a deep breath and let the rest of the sentence tumble out between them. "… and that you might be the father."

And then he was falling down, down, deep into his own mind while Christine's statement echoed all around him. Father. The foreign word held no meaning or place in his life until this moment.

His memories dragged him back to his childhood. He caught only a brief glimpse of his mother's repulsion as she looked at him, before another swift memory intruded—the same woman snatching a small bag of coins from a filthy gypsy man and walking away without a backward glance for her little son. No father appeared in those two memories. And no kindly older man and his wife appeared to welcome him into his new life with the gypsies. That only happened in fairy tales or to children born without disfigured faces. Only merciless beatings and revolted glances guided his life; only solitude embraced him when he woke weeping in the night.

And yet the word stoked at an unspoken longing within his

heart. Father. To have a child to love, to teach, to hold; Erik could almost feel the sweet warmth of cradling a babe in his arms. The child would not be flawed either; he or she would not suffer the devil's mark, and Erik vowed he would pray on his knees until the day Christine gave birth to ensure that. These feelings amazed him, his life amazed him, the life which had been forever shrouded in cursed shadow now contained so much blessed light. He could be a good father; he *wanted* to be a father!

Before he could share this revelation with Christine, who stood so anxiously, eyes wide and worried, Erik recalled another word, a word that drove a heavy fist into his gut. Might. He *might* be the father.

He imagined a beautiful baby with downy, blond hair gurgling merrily up at him. He felt a sickening fury rise up toward this image, threatening to engulf the innocent child. The innocent child. No matter if Raoul or himself were the father, this untainted babe would enter the world and need parents who loved him without question. Erik fought his fury and used every ounce of his will to block out the idea of Raoul sharing Christine's bed. During this internal struggle Erik won his final battle against his darkness.

He could not undo the past; the reaction he gave to Christine right now would determine the course of their lives. She loved him; he suffered no doubt of that. How very afraid she must be coming here with news of such emotional magnitude. How very brave of his marvelous Christine. Everything else receded, leaving only a picture of Christine and the babe smiling at him, safe and happy.

Though they stood indoors, Erik swore he felt the warmth of the sun bathing his face. Then he heard his old friend's voice within his heart and mind. *"This is your time now, my son. All that you deserve has come to pass. Be loved."*

Erik pulled Christine to him and let his absolute conviction infuse his voice. "Christine, my heart holds no place for the word 'might'. Have I no blood ties to this child, I can still be the very best of fathers. I want nothing more than that chance."

"Y-you are sure of this, Erik?" Christine's voice grew thin and watery.

Erik knew she teetered on the edge of falling apart. The unexpected plummets and the steep climbs of Christine's life were taking their toll, and up to this instant, she had shown more resilience than most. But now, she had no need to rely only on herself for strength. She had him. Erik rested her head over the steady beat of his heart. "I am sure, Christine."

Christine stayed abed the next few days at Erik's insistence. Now, feeling restored and restless, Christine decided to return to the school on the morrow rather than aimlessly wander Madame's apartments for another day. Save for Erik's afternoon visits and Madame's company at night, Christine felt quite alone and a little scared.

More often than not she would find herself resting her hand over her belly in a timeless pose. A life grew inside her, and while that thought filled her with wonder, the awful feeling of not knowing if the child were created in love or pity ate away at Christine's peace of mind. She wanted to treat this pregnancy as a blessing. But how could she when, if she could not get a divorce from Raoul and marry Erik, the child would then bear the label of bastard? This babe, only the tiniest flicker of light within her womb, already carried the yoke of its parents' emotional burdens.

Erik, however, seemed oblivious to these problems in the excitement of his impending fatherhood, and Christine did not have the heart to discuss Raoul and the matter of divorce. When she broached the subject of the child being a bastard, Erik became incensed.

"Will we ever know peace, Christine?" Erik's face burned dark and foreboding as he averred. "The Vicomte will divorce you and our child will not bear a stigma of any kind. Though you do not say it, I know the fear that lives inside of you…if a de Chagny has to die, it will not be you."

Christine grew alarmed. "Erik, do not say such things. I would not see Raoul dead anymore than I would see any one of God's creatures killed. We are not bringing an innocent babe into this world with a legacy of unending violence. We must find another way." Again, Christine rested her hand over her stomach, a hand that trembled.

Contrite, Erik gathered her up against him. "I am sorry. It would seem I have not begun to plumb my protective instincts when it comes to you and our child. I do not wish for bloodshed. Yet the Vicomte will have to listen to reason; I will give him no choice."

"Promise me that you won't hurt him, Erik. I would have your vow." Christine made sure she looked directly into the depths of his eyes—to his soul—as he gave his answer.

"You have my vow, Christine."

Madame Giry returned from the school, her presence a distraction from any further discussion of Raoul. In hindsight, it was a distraction at a terrible cost.

The clear day gave way to a foggy night as Raoul watched the school. He needed to see Christine, and believed that, like most things awaited long enough, a chance would present itself.

Opportunity arrived in the form of Christine stepping out the small side door of the church. Parked around the side of the building, Raoul would not have noticed her if he hadn't gotten out of his carriage to stretch his legs. He waited a few minutes to ensure no one followed after her and then crossed the expanse of grass, swiftly and stealthily.

Eyes closed, she sat on the bottom step of a small flight stairs that led from the school into a cobble-stoned courtyard lined with benches. A breathtaking statue of an Angel, wings outspread, face serene, hands in prayer, hovered in the corner.

As he approached, Raoul's eyes remained riveted on her. "Christine." His voice sounded harsher than he intended.

Her eyes blinked open, and she pulled herself up by the railing to a standing position.

Raoul emerged from the thickening fog. "Christine," he repeated. The panic he saw in her eyes dismayed him, and he felt the stirrings of anger as she glanced up toward the door to the school. "The monster is inside, not standing in front of you. You have nothing to fear from me."

"What are you doing here, Raoul?" Christine clenched the railing.

"I wanted to see you, to talk to you. I have been waiting outside of the school for the chance to catch you without some sort of guard."

Christine shivered a bit. "I came out here for some fresh air," she said in such a regretful tone that Raoul was offended.

"So, you do not wish to speak with me? I am your husband; did you think you could just walk away from our life and that would be an acceptable way to live?" Raoul took a step closer to Christine, and watched as she gripped the railing tighter and pulled slightly away.

"It's been a month, Raoul. You look hale and fit, not much like a husband who misses his wife." A flash of guilt crossed his face and Christine pressed him. "Why the sudden need to see me?"

Raoul did not answer right away. He looked at Christine with new eyes and realized he did not know this woman. He did not remember her ever being this way, so forward, so defiant. It had taken him a week to recover from his fight with the Opera Ghost, and afterward Raoul had thrown himself back into the social whirl of Paris. He thought of all the attractive, pleasant girls he had escorted about and how much he had enjoyed himself.

Perhaps he would have gone on in this manner, blocking out the reality of his marriage, continuing the charade of having a sickly wife. But lately he had endured nightmares from which he woke in a chilled sweat, the sound of a baby's cry lingering in his mind. He believed that mewling child to be the heir he would never have, and Raoul knew he could not go on with his performance, no matter how much he wished otherwise.

He was happier without Christine; that much he would admit to himself. She was not the wife he had dreamed to have by his side, nor did she appreciate him as a husband. Yet, the notion of her truly loving that murdering creature gnawed at his insides. He could not separate himself from the fury and resentment when it came to Christine and the Opera Ghost. Raoul wondered what objective answers he could produce for his failed marriage if he were able to think clearly on this matter. But he could not, and he *would not* allow the Opera Ghost to win. For that reason above all else, he refused to let Christine go.

"Raoul, it is cold and damp out here. You are correct in saying that we have much to talk about. But this is not the time nor the place." Christine's teeth were beginning to chatter, and she pulled her shawl snugly across her shoulders.

Raoul's eyes narrowed. "When would be the right time, Christine? When you have your monster by your side? I think we should continue this conversation in my carriage." He reached for her hand, but Christine looked at him nervously and shook her head. She evaded his reach, taking two of the steps closer to the church door.

Raoul dropped his hand slowly and gave Christine a look of profound hurt. "You would not go with me, Little Lotte? Has it come to this? Afraid to be alone with the boy you once played with in the attic?"

Christine bit her lip anxiously, her eyes filled with sympathy and sorrow. "I am sorry, Raoul. I did not mean to give the impression that I fear you. We will talk, but as I said, this is not the time or the place…and truly I am not feeling well. Erik will come looking for me any moment now, and I do not wish for more bloodshed."

At the mention of the Opera Ghost's given name, Raoul bounded up the steps and grabbed Christine's arm. "You are on such intimate terms, then?" he hissed.

"No, no we are not!" But Christine had eyes that could not lie, and she saw with dawning horror that Raoul knew it too.

His expression veered from plain anger to black hatred in an instant.

She wrenched her arm away and bolted up the steps. "Erik! Madame! Help me!"

"You are coming with me, Christine, and I shall let you rot in an asylum!" Raoul grabbed at her shawl and caught a fistful of the fabric as she reached the top step. He jerked her backward against him, but the knot loosened. Christine's feet slipped out from under her. She fell forward; the cruel, cold edges of the stairs slamming into her stomach and knocking the wind out of her.

As she tumbled down the rest of the flight, Christine felt the absence of her babe in her soul before she even hit the ground.

Raoul raced down the steps, crying her name.

When he reached Christine, the loathing in her gaze warned him not to touch her. Her entire being overflowed with anguish. She whispered one sentence, "You are the monster now, Raoul," and fell unconscious.

An inhuman sound of pain filled the night. Raoul glanced up to the steps in time to see a large, caped figure bearing down on him. He was brutally shoved aside as the Phantom gently picked up Christine's crumpled body and cradled her in his arms.

She stirred and pushed herself against his warmth, tears running down her still face.

Raoul remained on the ground staring up at Erik defensively. "She is my wife, I meant her no harm!"

"She was pregnant. Did she tell you?" Erik could feel a warm dampness from Christine's skirts seep through his sleeve. He knew she was now losing blood, and he began taking the steps rapidly.

Raoul struggled to his feet and called after him. "I did not know Christine is with child!"

At the top of the steps, Erik turned, Christine tight in his protective embrace. An expression of rage and condemnation suffused Erik's features, so powerful that Raoul took a step backwards.

"I said Christine *was* pregnant," Erik intoned, his voice shot with grief. He threw open the door, bellowing Madame Giry's name.

Raoul stared after them, his eyes empty, then dropped to his knees.

"I am a good man, I am a good man." He wept into his hands.

Chapter 29

CHRISTINE thought them angels; the faces of Meg, Madame Giry and Erik hovered in and out of her mind with blurred surrealism. Unaware that she opened her eyes from time to time and blearily focused on each person who gazed down at her, a vision of love and concern, Christine wondered why her angels looked at her with such worry? Each time the answer began to take shape in her mind, a dull ache began in her heart and burned down to her belly. Christine always shut her eyes before complete awareness set in. She sought refuge in the infinite darkness of slumber; while she slept nothing terrible could happen again, and nothing was real.

Madame cast a worried glance at Erik. He suffered as well, and the only person who had ever been able bring any comfort to him lay in her bed, silent as death. Madame watched as Erik held Christine's lifeless hand; he rubbed his thumb in tiny circles within her small palm. Not a word had passed his lips since he laid Christine against the pillows, so his voice, when he spoke, came as a surprise to Madame Giry as it cut into the thick silence of the room.

"It has been four days, Madame. Did the doctor say this would happen?"

"I know only what I told you before. He said she is young and she is healthy. But he cannot foretell if her spirit will heal along with her body. If Christine does not have the will to rejoin us, then there is nothing he can do." Madame's voice was helpless.

She felt her daughter lay a comforting arm around her shoulders and gave Meg a grateful look.

Meg had been observing Erik without his notice; this was the first time in her life that she had been this close to him, and she grew confused. This was the morally savaged creature whom everyone feared? He did not wear his mask, he did not have on his impeccably groomed wig, he had thrown his cape aside in a haphazard heap, and his clothes were in disarray. Yet the love and light that poured from him as he gazed at Christine took Meg's breath away, and for the first time in her life she knew true beauty—and now found peace with the assurance of such beauty.

This glorious archangel, who stationed himself so devotedly by Christine's side, would never let her die. Meg knew without a doubt that this man's soul would endure whatever hell he had to in order to save Christine, if it were necessary. This love aspired to heaven and beyond.

With a subtle gesture, Meg drew her mother toward the door.

"Christine will need more broth," Erik said without looking away from her face.

"Of course," Madame answered, and Meg closed the door behind them.

Erik could stand it no longer. He needed to do something. Every hour that passed felt more as if he mourned Christine rather than waited for her to awaken. He could not just sit and stare at her unmoving form and pale, waxy skin. To do so another minute would surely extinguish his faith in her recovery. He needed to reassure himself that she lived. Erik leaned in and placed his lips over Christine's, kissing her with tenderness that belied the strength of his need to crush her against him and force her to consciousness.

"I need you, Christine. Please, wake up." Erik let his fingers tangle in her long hair; he spread each curling lock about her with meticulous absorption, and then curved his large hand against Christine's cool cheek. "You must choose again…shall it be the gray specter of death or your devoted Phantom that calls your soul to his realm? Choose me, Christine. Death can wait until our lives are fulfilled."

Erik stared at his love, crooning softly to her, mindful to keep his voice strong and his song even lest it reach her heart unworthy.

"This unseen foe called black despair
Holds you in his desolate lair,
And I will fight as your devoted knight
To reclaim my sweet, Christine

Past my reach your will grows weak
The heart calls, though your lips won't speak
And I'll respond, ever strengthening our bond
Then shall hold my sweet, Christine

Come back to me, my breath, my life
To have and to hold as my cherished wife
And I will wait and defy this fate
And love my sweet, Christine.

To know your love, then lose its song
I will not be able to carry on
And I will die with one last sigh
Of your name, my sweet Christine."

Erik gathered Christine against him and rocked her while hot tears coursed down his cheeks. Her head fell limply against his shoulder and he kissed her cool forehead again and again.

"Do not give up, Christine. We have just begun; we have just found each other. For that reason alone, return to this world. Let me show you how much joy we have in store. I beg of you, open your eyes."

Erik pulled away to study Christine's face for any signs of movement but saw none, save for the occasional flicker of her eyelids as she dreamed.

He kissed her bloodless lips and whispered against them. "What do you dream of, Christine? Do you dream of the child that we have lost or the child that will be born to us?"

The sluggish pulse in Christine's neck quickened at his words. Erik pulled her closer and spoke fervently. "We will create another child, Christine, a beautiful, laughing child who has a guardian angel…our first babe. Think of it; a family is our destiny. Do not deny yourself that, do not deny me, for if you choose to slip away, then I must follow."

Christine's eyes fluttered, and Erik's heart leapt. His lungs filled with air as he waited for another indication that she heard him. But she did not stir again, and Erik released his breath through choking disappointment. "It is all right. When you are ready, I shall be right here."

Holding Christine against his heart lent a small measure of comfort; Erik allowed fatigue to weight his lids. He drifted off to sleep, searching for Christine in his own dreams.

Some time later, a small movement brought him wide-awake; Christine's fingers crept around his hand and held it. Her voice held no strength, yet its content made a profound impact. "I am ready."

"Christine!" Erik reveled in the sight of her wan smile, the most perfect of smiles she had ever bestowed on him. He reached over and plucked a half-filled glass of water from the nightstand, pouring small amounts through her thirsty lips just as he had done the past four days.

When Christine had drunk her fill, she pushed the glass aside. "Erik, I had the most blessed vision when I heard you speak of our lost babe."

Erik tucked her head underneath his chin, and closed his eyes, savoring the feel of Christine as her will to live returned and warmed her body. "I should like to hear this, if you feel able."

"Yes, I do," Christine whispered. "It is important that I share this with you before I lose the precious details. I'll start with my Grandmother; she was the most perfect grandmother a young girl could ask for. She gave me tea parties and stories and dress-up and secrets, but most of all she gave me her unconditional love, and I have never lost that feeling of being loved so wholeheartedly by her."

Christine's voice grew hoarse. Erik brought the glass to her lips and tipped more water through them. At her nod, he placed the glass down and listened to the rest of Christine's story.

"When I was six, she became very ill and at times forgot that she had been confined to her bed and could no longer walk. On her last day upon this earth, as I sat with her, stroking her white, soft hair, she said she would like to go on a picnic the next time I visited. I knew then that the angels would come to take her soon, and that this would be my final time with Grandmother in this life." Christine's voice trailed off and she gripped Erik's hand.

"Christine, this can wait, if it is too difficult."

"No." She cleared her dry throat and increased her grip. "I shall finish. I held my grandmother's hand much as I do yours now and assured her in a happy tone that we would indeed have a picnic. With her eyes closed, she could not see how I silently wept. Then she smiled and said, *'It does not take much; all you need is a large blanket and a big tree to spread it under.'* Those were the last words I ever heard her speak." Erik started to talk, but Christine stopped him.

"When your love broke through the wall I had built around myself, you let the light back in. When you spoke of our next child, I began to feel once more. But when you spoke of our unborn babe as a guardian angel…I saw my grandmother sitting on a large blanket underneath the shade of an enormous oak tree with our darling baby, and they smiled at me. I knew it was time to come back to you."

Erik looked up to the heavens and held his soul mate as if he would never let her go. "I am so glad, Christine."

She stirred in his arms and struggled to sit up. "How long have I slept?"

"Four days. You need to eat something and regain your strength." Erik lifted her with ease and lay Christine back down in her bed. "I will inform Madame and Meg that you are awake."

"Only four days have passed since I fell down those stairs?" She swallowed with some difficulty and regarded Erik for a moment before speaking. "I will need to regain my strength quickly. There is a matter of divorce that needs to be resolved at once." Christine's sweet voice now contained the arctic edge of a sharp blade.

Erik had never before seen hatred in Christine's eyes, and although he grieved for the loss of her innocence, he knew no one entered and returned from hell unscathed.

Chapter 30

RAOUL had gone underground. He did not deem himself worthy of his peers any longer, and if he could have found a lower form of life than the gaming hells and taverns he began to frequent, he would have wallowed in that refuse instead.

Gone was the debonair Vicomte; in his stead existed a broken, pitiful, carcass of a man whose mind burned with only one thought: Christine.

Raoul tortured himself with countless memories of her. He would watch them play out in his mind, always starting with the promising enchantment of the giggling young girl she had been and ending with the devastating renouncement of his soul from the woman who had suffered a brutal loss under his hand.

She had been carrying a child, and he could not feel any sadness over the loss. *Not when it could have been that fiend's offspring.* The voice inside his head shamed Raoul, forced him to acknowledge the ugliness in his soul and the truth of Christine's last words to him.

But what if it had been yours? This voice caused endless pain and rekindled his rage. If Christine had not been such a traitorous harlot they could have joyfully awaited their first child.

The heavily built barkeep ambled over to offer Raoul a refill of his ale, and then walked away shaking his head after he saw that the first mug had not yet been touched. Raoul never drank; he merely sat in whatever filthy establishment he found and thought himself into a stupor of self-loathing.

In his worst nightmares, he never imagined his life coming to this point. When he discovered Christine again after so many years, he thought he'd found his destiny in their love. He thought fate played matchmaker for the two of them alone. Why else would he find his way back into her life? *For what purpose did he serve if not to save Christine and earn her love?* This voice he hated most of all; for it changed the armed fortress of his existence into an empty house of cards. This voice shattered the Vicomte, and he still did not know the answer to the question.

He had always prided himself with the justification that Christine needed saving, that she needed his guidance; he never questioned her heart or whether she possessed any misgivings in the aftermath of their tumultuous engagement. If a kernel of doubt ever inserted itself into his mind, he quickly reminded himself that he was her savior and her childhood sweetheart. That he had rescued her from a distorted madman whose obsession with his own wants led to the ultimate sin of murder had only served to enforce his sense of righteousness.

A distorted madman whose obsession with his own wants led to the ultimate sin of murder. With stunned apprehension, Raoul lifted his eyes to stare at his dissolute reflection in the mirror above the shelves holding various liquors.

Every vile characteristic that he flung upon the opera ghost stared back at him, "Noooo!" Raoul hurled his glass at the mirror.

The mirror burst into sharp, splintered pieces that rained down over the bottles, the bar itself and all over the floor, but the image already branded itself into the very core of his being.

"You'd better be plannin' on payin' me for that." The barkeep lumbered to Raoul's end of the bar in an instant, his hostile expression showing he would enjoy taking his payment out by way of broken limbs.

Raoul tossed a heavy bag of coins onto the bar, indifferent to his near brush with danger. His boots ground into the shards of glass that sprinkled the floor as he made a quick exit, stepping through the door and onto the street.

For what purpose did I serve? he wondered in agony. Raoul did not move from the murky circle of light cast by a street lamp, unsure where to go.

The hairs on his neck suddenly bristled, and Raoul swung around to face the empty entrance to the tavern. He felt a threat in the air and was not indifferent to it this time. Fear filled his mouth with a metallic taste as he peered past the light and into the dense night.

"Vicomte de Chagny."

Erik appeared out of nowhere, his expression unreadable.

Raoul took an involuntary step back as he stared at his enemy. Impeccably attired as always, the Opera Ghost wore no mask. Startled, Raoul stared into the half-scarred face. Christine had chosen *this* over him? Christine. Suddenly a different sort of fear stopped Raoul's heart. "Is she…? Is Christine all right?"

In an instant Erik's hand rested on the hilt of his sword, and Raoul felt the lash of the other man's fury as Erik snarled, "Do not speak her name!"

"By the saints, I loved her, too! At least tell me if she is recovered."

Erik relented marginally. "She is." He released his grip on his sword and reached into his coat pocket. "These are for you. I had my lawyer draw them up." He handed a perplexed Raoul a sheaf of papers, rolled tightly and tied off in the middle.

Understanding replaced confusion, and Raoul sneered. "An Opera Ghost with lawyers? How absurd. These are divorce papers, I presume."

"Do not think to fight this, Vicomte. You owe it to her at the very least."

Raoul's crushing grip on the bundle put a warning glint in Erik's eye. "I will have them drawn up as many times as needed, though if you prefer you can do this at the tip of my sword. If you loved her as you claim, then give this to her." Erik enunciated the last four words.

"This will ruin my name. De Chagny's die before they divorce." Raoul held up his head proudly.

"Yes, well, unfortunately I made a vow that prevents me from fulfilling that assertion. Just sign the papers, Vicomte, lest I start thinking about the fact that I made that vow before you murdered her unborn child."

Now the voice that whispered inside Raoul's mind took on a face and form—one which he hated with every fiber of his being. The Opera Ghost forced Raoul to open his eyes and acknowledge the tragedy he had perpetuated. He leaned heavily against the wall of the establishment. "It was an accident. I swear I did not know what I was doing. I loved Christine so much and to lose her to what she begged me to save her from? I have known only shades of madness for months now."

Erik flinched at the reminder of Christine's defection. Minutes ticked by as both men reflected on the circumstances that had led them to this point, and then Erik offered Raoul two clipped words. "I know."

Raoul glanced up in surprise and found himself looking at *Erik* for the first time. How long had the humanity been there? And how long had his own been absent?

He straightened from the wall and gestured brusquely. "I will need my own lawyer to look everything over, and then I will send the signed papers on to Madame Giry's address."

Erik nodded. "We shall look for them."

A muscle ticked in Raoul's jaw at the word "we".

"You know you are still a wanted man. The end of my hunt for the Opera Ghost has not changed that." Raoul paused and then dared a question that he had longed to ask of Christine. "What kind of life can you give her?"

Erik waited a beat before responding, then spoke the words with soft assurance. "A life of song." He registered no surprise at Raoul's baffled look. "Good night, Vicomte."

Jealousy blazed in Raoul's heart. He did not understand what Erik spoke of, yet he knew intuitively that the man understood the composition of Christine's heart, one that Raoul himself could read, but never play. As Erik walked away, Raoul called out rashly, "And where is your mask tonight, Opera Ghost?"

The answer that he received silenced the voices and staggered the Vicomte de Chagny.

"I know my place in this world. I know my purpose."

A full sennight had come and gone before a sealed envelope with the de Chagny insignia stamped on the back arrived on Madame Giry's doorstep.

Erik took the envelope from the messenger, frowning at the slim feel of it. He ripped open the seal and removed a single sheet of paper.

Christine came hurrying out of the small parlor in the back. "Is that from Raoul? Did he sign the papers?" Excitement tinged her words.

Erik finished reading the letter and leveled hooded eyes at Christine. "He writes that he has had a change of heart and would like to meet with us."

"This can't be." Christine took the correspondence and studied the contents as if it were written in a language foreign to her. She looked up into Erik's troubled face. "I am frightened. Nothing good can come of it, Erik."

"If you do not want to go, then we won't. But, it would put an end to this never-ending nightmare once and for all."

She glanced down at the letter again and shook her head. "Why are you doing this, Raoul?"

Chapter 31

THEY arranged to meet in a small park that ambled along a river. More stone than grass, the area did not meet with favor from the citizens of Paris. Erik and Christine's driver pulled the horses to a stop a measurable distance ahead of Raoul's waiting carriage.

As Erik opened the door, Christine tugged on his arm. "Erik, forget about this. It pains me to say that I have no faith in Raoul any longer, but it is the truth."

Erik paused, taking Christine's hand within his own. "Tell me now if you want to leave. I will give the signal." He added, "At the cost of our freedom."

"Better our freedom than your life!" Christine searched Erik's eyes for signs of misgiving and only saw calm resolve. She drew strength from that and placed her hands on her lap, staring straight ahead. "I will wait and pray for this to be over soon. Keep your guard up."

Erik pressed a swift kiss on her mouth. "If I thought we could discover another way, Christine, I would seize it. I shall return shortly. Do not open this door for anyone other than myself." He stared hard at her distressed face and then was gone.

Only the moon illuminated the road as Raoul met Erik halfway between the carriages. The Vicomte scowled when he noticed Christine's absence. "This meeting has to take place with Christine as well."

"She is inside the carriage; you'll have to be content with that."

"I would see her, Phantom. If you wish things to proceed, then allow me a last moment." Raoul began slapping the gloves that he held against his thigh. "Please," he ground out.

"You will suffer if you upset her." Erik said, his voice as lethal as the blade at his hip. With an abrupt jerk of his head, he motioned for Raoul to follow him. Erik rapped lightly on the door when they reached the carriage. "Christine, the Vicomte is asking to see you, if that is a tolerable request."

She gave no answer, and nerves stretched in the prolonged silence. Finally the door opened and Christine stepped down with Erik's swift assistance. As her feet touched the ground, she cleaved to Erik's side at once, leaning into him and clutching his arm.

Raoul understood the significance of her actions, and he could only stare at his Little Lotte, while the pain in his heart stole the words from his mouth. She gazed at Erik much as she had gazed at himself that night on the roof of the Opera House, only now Raoul noticed a difference. The single flame of love that had shone in her eyes when she looked at her husband these past two years had been stoked into a blaze so brilliant it could rival the sun as she stared up at Erik.

Jaw clenched, Raoul spoke her name, bitterness coating the syllables. When she met his eyes, frigid contempt replaced the kind warmth he had always associated with her, and it stunned him. Still, Raoul expelled a sigh of relief. "You are well."

He hurried on at her incredulous look of anger. "Christine, you must know how remorseful I am. Even now guilt and sorrow muddle my senses and I cannot even begin to touch upon how I have wronged you. I tried so hard to fit you into my world. I tried to create a Vicomtesse out of an Angel...I see that now. But though I am a flawed man, I am also a man who can learn from his past mistakes. That dreadful night that I came to see you at the school, that is what I wanted to tell you. But then you informed me without words that you had lain with *him*."

Raoul shot a venomous look at Erik, who inclined his head, his derision evident. Raoul turned his attention back to Christine. "You chose him and betrayed our vows of marriage; moreover you betrayed my trust and my love. Do you know what that does to a man? Is the depth of my love shallow because you love him? Does it hold less value because you do not need it? Christine, I loved you."

Throughout Raoul's speech, Christine's face had softened. She took a step toward him and took his hand.

Erik's entire body tensed.

Raoul's eyes, hopeful and unsure, met Christine's sad gaze as she turned his palm so that it faced upward; the discordant chink of the Vicomtesse de Chagny's wedding rings sounding loud as they dropped into Raoul's hand. "I have no words left for you, Raoul. We have said our good byes."

The present has mirrored the past. Erik almost sympathized with the Vicomte at this moment—*almost.*

Raoul curled his hand around the rings, forming a fist. "So you do not find me worthy of redemption while his immoral deeds are exonerated by your love?"

Erik narrowed his eyes at Raoul's fist and made to shield Christine. She shook her head and addressed Raoul's contemptuous query.

"Every soul is worth redemption, Raoul, but we need to find it within ourselves before we look to others." Christine's voice contained a touch of pleading. "I hope that your actions tonight are an indication of your own healing. And I hope you know that I never would have loved you if I had not thought you a glorious soul to begin with." Christine turned away from her husband and let Erik hand her back into the carriage.

"I had to speak with him, Erik," she said in an undertone.

Erik nodded. "I did not expect differently." He shut the door with a light click, faced Raoul again and waited for his next move.

Raoul opened his hand and glanced down at the rings. Voice heavy, he said, "It is time." He motioned to his driver. The man thumped twice on the side of Raoul's carriage with the butt of his whip.

"What is this?" Erik demanded, his face thunderous.

Raoul gave Erik an enigmatic smile as two men climbed from

Raoul's conveyance. "I thought to secure witnesses to the abduction of my wife. One of them is the magistrate."

He yelled loudly as the men approached. "This man is the Opera Ghost, and he has taken my wife in that carriage!"

"Damn you, Vicomte!" Erik's anger rolled off his body in searing waves, but he did not move.

Raoul lifted a brow. "This is your one chance to run, Opera Ghost. You can be assured that I will be the first to find you." He cried out as a backhand from Erik sent him sprawling on the ground.

Erik threw open the door to his own carriage, shouting out to his driver to leave posthaste.

His team of horses whinnied noisily and the coach took off with a lurch. Erik swung himself into the seat opposite Christine while loud curses filled the night air behind them.

Christine stared him, her eyes wide and questioning. "What is going on?"

"He brought witnesses," Erik bit out.

"But why?"

"I assume so that they would bear proof of my demise. The fool!" Erik opened the door and peered back at the road behind them. He pulled himself back inside. "We have a good lead; we should be able to make it."

The coach swayed and bumped along the rutted street.

"This is madness." Christine whispered. "We should have known better than to trust him."

"It was not a matter of trust, Christine, it was a matter of starting a new life, free of the shackles of our past. We had no choice." Erik glanced out the window as the scenery raced past his vision. "Perhaps my need to call you wife has obscured my concern for your safety."

Christine took in a deep, calming breath. "I am acting foolish; I wanted this freedom as much as you and for the same reason. Someday, we will look back upon this night and laugh about our wild carriage ride through Paris."

Erik smiled at Christine, his eyes soft. "Yes, darling, we shall do that."

One of the wheels slipped into a particularly deep rut causing the carriage to bounce with jarring impact. Christine let out a small scream as she was thrown against the seat.

Erik leaned forward and helped her into a sitting position. "Are you all right?"

Shaken, she nodded, her eyes widening again in alarm as the sound of pounding hooves approached. In a flash Erik reached the back door, and peered out. Two men on horseback closed the distance rapidly; he made out the form of Raoul riding hard, only paces behind the magistrate.

Erik snarled in impotent fury as he saw the man raise a gun, aiming at the carriage.

A wild yell issued from the Vicomte. "For God sake man, put down the gun, my wife is in there!"

Erik ducked back inside and jerked Christine to the floor as the first bullet shot through the back window and out the front of the carriage.

The shriek of the frightened horses drowned out Christine's second scream. The vehicle plunged ahead and the two rolled haphazardly on the floor. Erik wrapped his body around Christine, protecting her from slamming against the footrests.

Another shot was fired. A grunt of pain issued from the driver as he toppled from his perch and onto the ground. The carriage swayed wildly and the horses veered off the road across a wide expanse of grass, perilously near the river. Christine sobbed out her fear.

"Christine!" Erik's voice was urgent as he held her close. "We are on a death ride now, the horses are out of control." Christine began to shake, and Erik gripped her hand. "We will have to jump. I think we have gained some distance with the horses on uncharted terrain. With luck our cursed pursuers will not see us and continue to chase the carriage. Are you ready?"

Christine nodded against him, not trusting herself to speak. Erik moved with resolute speed as he brought Christine to her feet. The coach bucked and he braced their bodies against the violence of the ride.

Her hand gripped his with strength lent by terror. Christine stared at him as tears welled in her eyes. "Do not let go of my hand," she wept.

"Never." He vowed, then threw open the door.

They registered the blur of ground beneath them, the river beyond, and the thick forest that loomed up ahead and then gazed back at each other with resolution.

"I love you, Erik."

"Outside of eternity." Hands clasped, they leapt from the racing coach.

Time slowed as the two fell. Erik noted the jagged rocks that thrust up from the grass and once again used his body to shield Christine. His head absorbed the blow that would have been hers. Christine cried out as she crashed against Erik's body and rolled off him. Greedy oblivion swallowed her mind.

Raoul found them lying there, hands still locked together. He rushed to Christine and crouched beside her, saw that she still breathed, then moved to Erik's lifeless body and felt for a pulse.

He smiled in satisfaction as the magistrate and his officer rode up and called out, "The Opera Ghost is dead, gentlemen. The city of Paris can sleep safely now."

Before the men reached him, Raoul turned back to the couple and yanked their hands apart, a slight sneer curling his lip.

He stood up and brushed himself off.

One of the men looked at Christine lying so still on the ground. "And your wife?"

Raoul stared at her as well and grief roughened his voice. "I am afraid she will not last much longer. This ordeal will surely have her dead by morning." He crouched down and lifted Christine up carefully while the men looked on in sympathy.

"What should we do with him?" The magistrate inquired, jerking his chin at the prone figure of Erik.

"Let the fishes have him; I do not want his blood staining my fine carriage. Nor do I want the coroner involved. My family's name has suffered enough." Raoul nodded at the magistrate. "See that it is recorded that the Opera Ghost is no longer…without involving myself or my wife, and I will fund your political aspirations."

The man's eyes lit with avarice and he nodded back.

"We have a deal then. Now, if you two will go back and take care of the driver's body, I will do the honor of disposing of this one." Raoul used his booted foot to shove Erik's form; it rolled down the small hill into the darkness and toward the river. Long seconds passed before they heard a large splash. The magistrate and the officer rode off laughing.

Christine let out a small whimper in Raoul's arms, but she did not wake. His carriage pulled up on the embankment and Raoul trudged toward it. "Do not fret, my Little Lotte, you shall be with your precious Erik soon enough," he murmured darkly.

One month later…

The Vicomte de Chagny stood at his wife's grave in the cold autumn air. The trees that scattered around the cemetery held scant leaves on their branches, and the wind blew hollowly through them.

Raoul stood as still as the stone markers that surrounded him. "I have met someone, Christine. A girl who knows my world, as she was born to it as well. And she makes me smile, something I have not done in a long while."

Raoul emitted an empty, self-depreciating laugh. "I am not sure why I came here to tell you this. Perhaps I feel vindicated that someone loves me, that she has seen something worth loving within me and thus proved to me that I deserve such love. You were correct when you said I needed to find redemption within my own heart first."

He placed a small posy of forget-me-nots in front of her gravestone and straightened, soft tears streaking his cheeks. "I never intended to cause you such loss. I will harbor that crushing regret until I die. I wish I were not standing in front of a slab of stone talking to you as if you can hear me. Strange as it may seem,

I feel close to you here. I feel that you finally listen to me."

"I do not think I will love this girl as I loved you; my heart doesn't have that to give anymore. Nor do I think it could love anyone with the completeness that I did you." Raoul pulled his coat closer around his body and walked against the biting wind that carried his words across the empty graveyard. "I don't want to."

Madame Giry sat before her mirror, adding the last pin to her chignon. Tonight the school celebrated its opening. Never had she imagined what a drastic turn her life would take in the course of a month. With a pang in her heart she thought of how different the opening of the school would have been if the Vicomte hadn't interfered in their lives.

Madame pushed down the annoying lump in her throat. She had become increasingly sentimental of late and feared that she would burst into tears when she set foot inside the school that night. She took a calming breath to steady herself and then got up to retrieve a thick cloak from her closet. Suddenly she wished she had someone to accompany her and thought wistfully of Meg, who would join her mother at the party, along with her new husband.

A light rap sounded on her front door, and Madame hurried to answer it. Ducray waited on her doorstep, dressed as fine as any lord. Madame Giry gaped at him.

"Ducray, what are you doing here?"

The customary twinkle missing from his eyes, he gave a slight bow and offered his arm. "I thought you could use the company tonight, Madame."

The annoying lump had returned. Madame slowly linked her arm through Ducray's. "You are correct, Monsieur. Tonight I could certainly use your company."

From the Vicomte de Chagny,
  It would seem that I have experienced a change of heart. After dwelling on many things these past days, I have come to one conclusion.
  Divorce will never work, and Christine deserves far better than to live with a hunted man, the happiness of freedom forever denied to her. You were correct in that, Opera Ghost; I do owe her that at the very least.
  So, I propose your deaths. I shall meet with the two of you at a park that is not too far from the school. And from there, we shall stage the Opera Ghost's abduction of my wife that will result in a fatal carriage accident. It is a simple plan, and not without benefit to myself. My life will be my own again, and I shall endeavor not to make the same mistakes twice. I am working out the details of proving your deaths at the moment; we shall need some way of recording the fact that the Opera Ghost is dead.
  Though I hate the thought of losing Christine to a man for which I harbor only loathing, Yet, I hate the thought of what I have turned into since entering your lives two years ago even more. I would like to gaze into the mirror again and respect the man staring back. I would like to silence the voices that question the kind of monster I have become.
  If you wish this meeting to take place, respond immediately by way of messenger. This decision did not come easily, so I will thank you to assist me in expediting this course of action as soon as possible.

The letter from the Vicomte to Christine and Erik lay in the bottom of Madame Giry's drawer. She kept it as proof of something that she had known since the day she spirited away the young boy with a disfigured face. Though she never shared the letter with Meg, Madame had shared her wisdom.

"We are all capable of great light or great darkness, no matter if you possess the face of an angel or the mask of a demon. There are circumstances beyond our control that can draw out an evil within ourselves; one that we never knew existed. But in the end, there is always hope for redemption."

One year later...

Christine sat at her secrétaire by an enormous window with a magnificent prospect of the gardens and sifted through the day's post. She smiled happily when she saw that both Meg and Marie de Ripon had written her. Excited to hear news of Paris and the school, she chose Meg's letter first. Christine let out a soft laugh as she read her friend's correspondence.

"What has you so amused?" Erik walked into their bedroom, smiling.

Christine continued to read while she gave him her absent answer. "Meg has just informed me that your butler decided to propose to Madame Giry in front of all the students. Her response was to hit him over the head with a violin and chase him out of the school."

Erik winced in sympathy of Ducray.

Christine laughed again. "Yet now Madame wears a lovely sapphire on her ring finger, though she refuses to talk about it. Do you think it is time we return to Paris, Erik? I confess I feel guilty resting out here in the countryside while Madame has the entire school to contend with. We left so quickly after the opening."

"She is in her element, Christine, and you have just given birth.

We are all where we are supposed to be." He crossed to Christine and traced the curve of her cheek. "At last."

"At last," Christine echoed, her eyes shimmering with joy.

Both thought back to the night of the carriage ride and how close they had come to death. Raoul's plan had been a simple one, but even the simplest of plans went awry.

The sound of a baby's cry filtered into the room. Christine rose from her chair, but Erik shook his head.

"Finish your letter; I will see to our son."

He strode into the peaceful nursery, to the bassinet where his child lay, fussing and babbling his indignant misery to the world.

"Shhh, D'Artagnan, shhh." Erik picked up his baby and cradled him tenderly. D'Artagnan calmed and looked at his father with such satisfaction that Erik shook his head with amusement. "So, we are here to serve you, young master? To fill your life with wonder and love and music and laughter?"

He crossed to an open window and stared out to the world beyond, then gazed back down at his beloved child. "I will see to it, my son," he whispered softly. "I love you."

The warm rays of the sun bathed the baby's smooth, beautiful face in golden light as he smiled up at his father, his soulful eyes mirroring the sentiment.

Love can cost you your soul, but it could also bring it back again.

The End

To order additional copies, please go to
www.phantomreturns.com

or contact
JimSam Inc. Publishing

at
www.JimSamInc.com

or
813-748-9523